CW00801216

AGENTS OF OBLIVION

Agents of Oblivion

by

Iain Sinclair

Swan River Press
Dublin, Ireland
MMXXIII

Agents of Oblivion
by Iain Sinclair

Published by
Swan River Press
at Æon House
Dublin, Ireland
August MMXXIII

www.swanriverpress.ie
brian@swanriverpress.ie

Text © Iain Sinclair
Illustrations © Dave McKean
This edition © Swan River Press

Cover design by Meggan Kehrli
from artwork by Dave McKean

Typeset in Garamond by Steve J. Shaw

Paperback Edition
ISBN 978-1-78380-771-0

Swan River Press published
a limited hardback edition of
Agents of Oblivion in May 2023.

Contents

Lifting a smoky glass to

B. CATLING

Poet, painter, performer, friend.

Agents of Oblivion

"*Then the river writhes in revulsion, its current flowing backwards, washing the dead back into life.*"

– *Franz Kafka,* The Aphorisms

Code 4: Agents of Oblivion

"Generally speaking the dead do not return," Artaud pronounced in a prose poem called "Electroshock", composed after his involuntary transit from Dublin to the tender care of French asylums. Chains. Straitjacket. Convulsions. No return to any of his earlier selves. Artaud was a seeker but there was nothing economic about his migration. The dead are permitted to visit those who welcome them. Their spectral, machine-made voices echo in deep tunnels under London. Voices without hosts. Without agency. They make their oracular pronouncements even when nobody is listening on the vast empty platforms of the Elizabeth Line. They have their codes and their secret meanings.

Code 4 alerts transport operatives to an unspecified violation: "spillage". It is not blood or shit or vomit, this time. Narrative spillage. Ghost stories leaking through a permeable membrane between remembered experience and high fiction, between the living dead and the unquiet residents of other dimensions. Sleepwalking voyagers are on the drift, tapped by angels, prodded by demons. They are known as "Agents of Oblivion". They do not possess badges or guns. And they did not take their inspiration from a defunct swamp rock combo of the last millennium. But there are no coincidences in the city of shadows. Four stories starting everywhere and finishing in madness. Four acknowledged guides. Four tricksters. Four inspirations.

Blackwood. Machen. Ballard. Lovecraft. Spillage on the line. God's face is pressing against a suburban window. We are becalmed in crisis. Phones twitter like starlings. Books are burning.

THE LURE OF SILENCE

"Silence, cooked like gold, in / charred / hands."

– Paul Celan

Resurrecting myths of a lost childhood, Blackwood promoted afresh the story of the ladder against his bedroom window. A workable symbol derived from Jung or Egypt or some picture book encountered on one of his long tramps through dark places, inns in German forests, wilderness cabins in Canada. His biographer Mike Ashley tells us that the author "warned against ever camping on the edge of anything". Never sleep on the imaginary line between woods and open country. Algernon understood all too well "the power and psychology of a single location" and the inevitable risks when the chosen site becomes "a frontier between our world and another".

In maturity, spotted bowtie secure, skull gleaming, the tall man was a consummate public performer, needing no written prompts. The grinding New York poverty of youth, as much as late success with a hissing radio microphone, too many cigarettes, too much London society endured and exploited, etched mortality into loosening folds of flesh. Pulsing temples are veined with blue worms. Wide eyes strain in dread that lizard skin will pouch. And seal those fading orbs. Casting the exhausted initiate into perpetual night and silence.

Starlight Man. Blackwood had silvered in the dish. Age induced a kind of vertigo. He was like an experienced climber who becomes suddenly conscious of self and abyss. And the impossible relationship between these two warring contraries. And who asks to be blindfolded. Involuntary memories return and are bent in the telling. He says that he crept out, in nightwear, barefoot, down that convenient ladder—*who set it there?*—into the thirty-acre garden, the family estate, towards a black pond. It was not this house, birthplace on Shooters Hill, with stables and conservatory. Or the gothic refuge in the woods, barred windows, double doors: private asylum for hiding away inconvenient lives.

That was something he could never expunge, the naked faces of those who had been imprisoned, as a financial scam, and held until they were driven mad. The terrified expressions on release when the police arrived with a posse of accompanying journalists, Blackwood amongst them. Shock. Horror of morning. The faces, he said, were tragic masks. Like carvings cracking at the tap of a hammer. Sunlight after years of wards and cells and shutters. Walls that did not sound when heads were beaten until brain mush ran out from the ears. Anguish frozen in a single exposure. The pain of recognition. The expression on Blackwood's own face when Bert Hardy came to take his portrait for a magazine.

The ladder. The unattended ladder.

The wooden ladder resting against a high window at the side of the house in the cul-de-sac, near the summit of Shooters Hill. That's what the young man, down from Newcastle, wanted to talk about. He was preparing a dissertation on that remarkable story by Alan Moore. "Unearthing" was a rhapsody, a fugue. A tribute to a friend, mentor, accomplice in ritual magic and mushroom-gobbling, roof-lifting derangement: Steve Moore. And to this location, the nexus of so many intersecting lives. Here was a premature obituary, lovingly crafted, roaming in free-flowing prose through a psychobiography of man and place. And arriving, just when it felt as if there were no way out, at an ending that could never be final. Steve is outside his crusty den, down the ladder—which was not yet in position—and frozen alongside the Shrewsbury Barrow, a modest Bronze Age burial tump. At which point, miraculously, the suburban adept, retired from his affiliation with the Illuminates of Thanateros (New Cross chapter), becomes the place, making literal what was always implied.

"You realise that the glasses are in fact a pair of dormer windows set into a housetop downhill, visible through parted trees that form the edges of his face, a patch of negative space strung across the gap between them," Alan Moore wrote.

We reel and spin. There are so many temporal and spatial superimpositions, so much doubling. More Moores than we can reasonably be expected to handle. The story is Alan's equivalent of Blake's "The Mental Traveller" from the Pickering Manuscript. "The trees bring forth sweet Extacy / To all who in the desart roam." Old forests form a choking ruff around the neck of the hill. "Unearthing" is cyclic: teacher becoming pupil, mentor becoming friend. Geological and historic records only confirm the novelty of the present moment. Which is gone before we know it has arrived.

Steve Moore accepts the limitations of a given family, education, love life, address. And he makes it mythical. He summons his namesake, Alan, to lift the tangled rootball of narratives to another dimension. His visitor recognises and records Steve's advent: "Stephen James Moore is born to a full moon on June 11th 1949, a crescent mark staining his forearm, there upon the crescent hill. Gemini, like his brother. Fire of air, the tarot Knight of Swords . . . His earliest memory is of September 20th the next year, 1950, fifteen months old, held up by his mother to look at a bright blue moon, this famous rarity occasioned by vast tracts of forest then ablaze in Canada."

Algernon Blackwood in his childhood bedroom recalled the face of god appearing, huge and round and blank, at the window. And then, as entertainer and rationalist, he offers the explanation: it was a barrage balloon, an anti-aircraft device, escaped its moorings. And still, within its featureless, window-smothering intrusion, its brushing against that particular pane of glass at that particular time, it was as much a deity as Steve Moore's moon.

I do not remember the book that fell on my head, gifting the yell of life. The smoke from burning docks. The extinguished town witnessed from an empty road as the doctor drove his pregnant wife to the private nursing home, a first child lost. I only remember and rearrange the stories. I know the date, June 11th. Six years before Steve took up residence at the summit of Shooters Hill. Decades before the twinned Moores, now ancient, now babes, became the Dr. Dee and Edward Kelley of workings in Northampton and the bachelor bedroom alongside old Watling Street. They exchange masks, these study partners. Exchange roles. The same thirst for the absolutes of knowledge. The raising high of the roof beams, carpenters.

When, in May 1997, I walked with Alan Moore to Mortlake, in quest of Dee's burial place, and when the journey was completed and Alan set aside the scrying glass and the bag of books, he called for a taxi, to carry him to Shooters Hill for a debriefing with Steve. That was the house at Hillend, the one that seemed to have been built, brick by brick around its lifelong occupant, around the room where it was destined to happen. A parking space was reserved, no doubt, for Harry Price, the dubious ghost hunter burlesqued by B. Catling in his Dorchester-on-Thames novella, *Munky*. And for future pilgrims attempting to identify the right semi-detached house. The lad, down from Newcastle, wondered if his sat-nav app would take him to the door. Or if, as he decided, with train services suspended and signalling down, rolling strikes everywhere, to call it a day. And to rely on internet searches and recorded interviews.

After our two-coffee-jug conversation, the student passed on some gossip that might have come from an acquaintance of Alan Moore or a documentary filmmaker whose portrait of Steve had been spiked and put in the vault along with several hours of abortive recordings with the Mole Man of Hackney. It seems that Steve had a prescient dream, in which he was tipped from his chair, to fall, infinitely slowly and forever, towards the floor, and through the floor, arms out, diving into darkness. A soft membrane over the Shooters Hill abyss. A vision that he recorded in his last journal.

In falling he remembered the face at the window. The scraping of a ladder against the sill. Which was, the student said, how he died. And how, when neighbours hadn't seen him making any of his regular circuits, they sounded the alarm. A builder's ladder was obtained. And Steve was found, slumped, as in his accurate premonition. After all, he was an acknowledged narrative craftsman. He knew how to storyboard and edit. You can't work up suspense until you know how it ends. But you are always hoping that you're wrong. It might have been a window cleaner or a man checking the roof for storm damage. Or clearing sodden leaves from a gutter.

During the weekend when Steve was still present in the back bedroom, the workspace, among his books, calm, dead, and undisturbed, several independent sightings were recorded. In the cul-de-sac. Out on the street. Drifting towards his favoured pub, The Bull. And looping around crescents—the lunar shape he honoured—towards the enclosed Bronze Age tumulus. It was as if he had been compelled to enact and confirm Alan's predicted conclusion in "Unearthing". Written is stronger than performed. They spoke, the witnesses, of a blue shirt. It was out of character. But Steve had chosen to wear it for the closing scene. And for two days afterwards, he appeared, to certain people at certain times. Not walking but moving around his usual places. He liked the discipline of routine.

He did not speak. He was an apprentice of that special local silence. Otherwise, a little paler of cheek, he was the same man.

When the student departed, burdened with hours to transcribe and with his previously solid thesis coming apart, he left me with a troubling gift: this tale of the man with whom I shared a birthday. Already a doubled and immortal fiction, Steve Moore was doomed (or privileged) to beat the bounds of Shooters Hill, in and beyond the moment of death. If ever there was a haunting for Blackwood to investigate, this was it. But if the affair was not to be a nicely contrived anthology piece or a radio chat in which irrational elements are played down, it would have to be accessed by way of Blackwood's "psychical" detective, Dr. John Silence. "For the cases that especially appealed to him were of no ordinary kind, but rather of that intangible, elusive, and difficult nature best described as psychical afflictions." I had no interest in, or gift for, pastiche. A non-canonical addition to the corpus of established Silence tales was not to be contemplated.

Blackwood's detective, as real as Holmes or Margaret Thatcher, existed only in territory that had already been mapped. But could he be contacted on the ground where his author had taken his first greedy breath? There was an obligation, in the John Silence stories Blackwood contrived, to deliver resolution. Sometimes these efforts were independent of the psychical detective and he was grafted on in a cameo role, in order to qualify some exotic travel piece for the brand. Without doubt, there were infinite legends of cases undertaken by the spook hunter unpublished. And unwritten. Sherlock Holmes goes on and on. Like a curse. Silence was always reluctant to play an active role in his own stories.

"You surely can't act death," J. H. Prynne tells us. Steve Moore refutes the claim. He acted death by being dead.

From the ground, I hoped to tease out the only man, available in any parallel dimension, to investigate the mystery of Steve Moore, as depicted (and therefore created) by Alan Moore. Silence, in a story called "A Psychical Invasion", confessed to a weakness for dubiously infested properties on the high ground of London.

"It all seemed so rapid and uncalculated after that— the events that took place in this little modern room at the top of Putney Hill between midnight and sunrise— that Dr. Silence was hardly able to follow and remember it all."

So it begins, somewhere undefined close to the second highest natural point in London. Nothing higher between the extinguished scribe, alone and rooted in Eaglefield Park, and Berlin. Between Steve Moore positioned by Alan Moore—who has anticipated everything—and whatever or whoever must be scattered, blown away, and lost as a grey-white snowfall of ash over the twilight Shrewsbury Barrow. In the enveloping dusk, London rain falls steady.

And mourners disperse to their interrupted tasks. It is done. It is just beginning.

Being rather than performing, or performing being, the traveller, himself a fictional device, sets out on his quest, to channel Dr. John Silence. Or to be absorbed into an unwritten history of Silence that can never be written by going deep underground, under the River Thames, by way of the Elizabeth Line: a line named after a dead queen, and celebrated in a newspaper cartoon in which the monarch, riding in frozen solitude, on tracks dedicated to her continuing glory, goes west, where the service does not yet run, along the horizontal steel ladder between Paddington and Reading, to attend her own obsequies. Before taking a specially constructed lift down into the cold vault beneath the private chapel of a private castle, paid for by a grateful but demanding public. They adore the fiction of history, of their own place in history, as proud victims. They love royals stepping through the rubble of Bethnal Green, wars and developers. They love royals at war, in and out of uniform, tilted with medals, plotting against each other. The most repellently obsequious of all the salaried Cotswold courtiers boasts of his abiding affection and respect by demanding that one of the tribe, young, female, alien, be stripped naked, to parade through the streets of our restored medieval heritage village while she is pelted with dung.

The traveller is feverish, between plagues, post-Covid, pre-variant, soon he will be separated from himself. He will be as a dead person, swimming backwards, on the wrong side of the river. Communicating still but unheard. In the way that he cannot help but hear the disembodied voice, belonging to no human entity, atypically clear, funnelling out over that long new platform, a street made as a future bomb shelter, where there are no other morning travellers, calling a Code Six incident. The traveller has worked at night, shifting mailbags, on these stations. He knows what that code means.

Nobody responds. The only uniforms are far away, more like reps for travel agents, primed to advise brave souls wheeling life's possessions towards some Heathrow terminal. Code Six has a double meaning: "responding from a long distance" and "litter". The distance must be equivalent to that between continents, between life lived and life in permanent cryogenic suspension. The recorded voice message is a robotic séance. The category of litter has not been specified, but the platform for Abbey Wood and Woolwich (where the traveller will disembark) is pristine. You could lick your proverbial all-day slop from it. *But, wait, somebody already has!* Steam rises as from a manhole cover. They should have called a Code Two. And sent for shovel and rubber gloves. Faeces, human, adult, recent, copious. In a broken line. Like tracks sniffed by a frontier scout. A dirty protest in a showcase environment, perhaps? Protesting about what? What have you got? Mainly, I suppose, the total absence of "facilities" for travellers, male or female, unless certifiably disabled, here at this major transport hub, where the limping, dragging, child-bearing, brave and doomed, and wrestling with bags and buggies, the serially incontinent with their families and carers, detrain for the new hospital complex. And how, as a necessary cost-cutting exercise made in support of grand projects, conveniences have been rationalised, re-visioned as bars or hair salons, padlocked, roller-shuttered against rough sleepers. Who are now obliged to piss against the walls. Uric stalagmites of repeat micturitions percolate into recent aerosol scribbles and signatures. In an impoverished section of Woolwich, on the end-wall of a rundown shopping parade, opposite one of the discontinued facilities for Gentlemen, there is an RA summer-show-quality spray paint portrait, super size, of a young black man, chin on fist, in contemplation. As if at stool, on a plain black chair. An invocation of Rodin or early gestural Cézanne. But in its placement, it looms like a satiric comment on the locked, twin-entry shed. A flaming orange background has been touched in and abandoned. Nightwalkers and homeless folk, alone or in couples, direct easing jets through the railings. And squat against the garages of the flats.

Our mental traveller, not yet referred to the Memorial Hospital on Shooters Hill, and not yet in direct communication with John Silence, Algernon Blackwood, or Alan Moore, strides around the Woolwich piazza—barracks, arsenals and weapon stores referenced and exorcised by novel conversions, familiar restaurant franchises and convenience stores (some with conveniences)—as he tries to orientate himself to the railway satellite, before nominating the best route for climbing the shoulder of the gravel-crusted clay slope, in the general direction of the eccentric redbrick water tower marking the proximity of Steve Moore's 1930s des-res retreat.

Dr. Silence, pointy chin resting on steepled fingers, would withdraw into reverie, reassured by the knowledge that "thought can act at a distance". There is no requirement to circumambulate the Woolwich parade square examining random artefacts, colonial plunder dressing commercial and cultural enterprises. The twin dogs, more doorstops than savage guardians like the pair on plinths in Victoria Park, stared across at the Elizabeth Line station entrance.

The other sculpture of note was not legible, but it might have found a place in Alan Moore's discussion of Steve Moore's abiding fetish: Artemis-Selêne. His muse, model and transdimensional love object. The slender, ice-veined moon goddess of the humped hill. This other lumpy Woolwich piazza figure, clearly the marker for our pilgrim walk, has an arm raised, hand amputated, to indicate direction of travel. Onwards and upwards. The votive being is gender non-specific, fashionably transitioning, wallowing in heavy pleated skirts that fall across powerful warrior thighs. The sculpture is magnificently distressed, features not so much erased as amplified in obscurity. Lichen to emphasise declivities. Fossil crusts. Threads of sympathetic vegetation picked up on the long voyage.

There is a bronze plaque with proud oxidised lettering: DEUS LUNUS. LATE ROMAN WORK. BROUGHT FROM EGYPT. Liberated, as ever, by the acquisitive military. A trophy god shaking a fist at the modest Shooters Hill massif and the residue of a straight Roman road. Deus Lunus is a mooncalf, as blank of expression as the floating god that banged against Blackwood's nursery window. This moulting plaster figure will never be devoured by the wolf of darkness, by the wolf of the woods. Time surgery has succeeded. The grafts, the plaster of Paris bandages, they bind dissolving bones. The scalpel of Dr. Silence is required, in order to reveal the cast of a blinding lunar beauty. The Egyptian moon is a pursuer. Deus Lunus bless our sneezing ascent.

Leaving the development zone, the traveller is at his ease. Within a few strides, he is reunited with reality. As he knows it. Eternal struggle. A man among men (and women), all unequal, on a wide pavement where the tribes of London continue to make their bitter best of the worst of it. Dying street markets with desolate stalls confirm their endurance, in rain, wind, and flapping canvas. They provide some solace for careful investors without cards to swipe. Old people labour to fill rescued plastic bags (branded by shops they have never entered). They struggle to scoop up bruised fruits and off-cuts of rank animals. Beggars, too cold to utter, take their turn to keep some small patch of pavement dry, beside a broken cash machine or a cut-price supermarket. Every steel shutter has its posters warning of climate change. THIS IS THE PRICE OF OIL. OCCUPY WESTMINSTER. But not on Sunday, when the Elizabeth Line is resting.

The first gentle gradient, up Burrage Road towards Plumstead Common, is an amiable portrait of managed entropy in the teeth of what has been imposed as conceptual fallout around all the stations of the new railway. Everywhere is five minutes from somewhere more desirable. Drudging uphill, inhabitants wrestle with bundles, with spare children and stuttering disability buggies. The battery has died on one old lady, but she's well placed, with a good view back down to the river. Walkers stop to talk. She is lively, asks for a cigarette, and says that when the doors open, someone will carry her across the road to Trinity Methodist Church and Youth Club, where scouts from the 4th Royal Greenwich, are handing out food parcels to a sociable queue. Making conversation with the pilot of the vehicle with the dead battery, an armour-plated Trumpist golf cart, the traveller could not help but be affected by a lengthy history of useless husbands, remembered wars, labours among other girls and widows in Woolwich armament factories. Like Alan Moore's vision of Steve at Shrewsbury Barrow, here was the face of a woman whose lineaments mapped a territory. It would be sentimental to think she belonged in an uncorseted reminiscence by Moorcock or Angela Carter. But she had that same vim, the sting of glottal demotic, like the magnificent Mrs. Cornelius and the

Chance sisters. Every other word a genteel obscenity, she never strayed towards the spiteful road rage of entitled seniors hogging the promenade in Hastings. The Burrage Road disability chariot reminded me of Blackwood's own experience of electricity, when he was obliged to explain the mechanics of a novel form of execution to condemned prisoners headed to Sing Sing.

"I could do without these memories, but they never fade. I can see the twitching features, the forced smile."

The narrating, as a journalistic duty, of the consequences of a hair-scorching and heart-stopping surge of high-voltage current prints an image that cannot be erased. This humane transit, from one hell to a worse, was invented by a New York dentist, and tested in tanks of water on hundreds of stray dogs, thus solving two problems at once. The effectiveness was confirmed when a thrill seeking drunk broke into a generating house and grabbed the brush and ground of a dynamo. He fried. Blackwood was there in town when street lighting revealed new prospects and inventors secured their monopolies.

Now cash was being offered for cars and vans: "in any condition". But there were no takers. The wasteground behind the fence was busy rewilding without council assistance. A blue plasterboard "Clearway" contradicted itself with warnings of "sharp spikes" and a formidable set of razor-honed spinners. An isolationist vision of Burrage Road as a barrier keeping out economic migrants, like a wall between Arizona and Mexico. Blackwood was quite right, frontiers are no place to make camp. The grudging hill had its own stream of clear water bubbling from a crack in the paving stones, rushing deliriously from overwhelmed or fat-blocked Victorian pipes. Water ran down to Plumstead Road, sparkling in shocks of sunlight between cooling showers.

Identifying Mayplace Lane, a narrow snaking track explored on many previous outings, put the traveller back in touch with the local grimoire, the force field of Steve Moore. Mayplace Lane was as unnaturally calm as Deadman's Walk in Oxford, that legendary passage of Jewish funeral processions. If the blue-shirted spectre of Steve was still beating the bounds, coming away from Hillend house and tumulus, this is the route he would take to the river. Where all the London dead float and sing, impervious to sewage outflow.

It wasn't the pollen, nor the dying abundance of winter, the mattress of leaves and wet wipes, but the feverish traveller was racked with sneezing. Veins hammered in his head. His ears rang. Mayplace was another border, the kind John Silence learned to exploit as a method for accessing higher states of consciousness.

"If you knew anything of magic," he improvised, "you would know that thought is dynamic, and that it may call into existence forms and pictures that may well exist for hundreds of years. For, not far removed from the region of our human life is another region where float the waste and drift of all the centuries, the limbo of the shells of the dead; a densely populated region crammed with horror and abomination of all descriptions, and sometimes galvanised into active life again by the will of a trained manipulator, a mind versed in the practices of lower magic."

The tunnel of the mulched narroway, disputed by trees and the tumbledown fences of back gardens, had been adapted as a cemetery of abandoned vehicles. The owners preferred to give them a decent burial, rather than claiming a few pounds from the breakers' yard on Burrage Road. Flat tyres sunk into the rich leaf mould. Insects colonised windscreen wiper blades and gaps in the radiator grille. Glass was smashed from the wing mirrors. There was a

Pharaonic grandeur, a chrome dignity, to these wrecks. Some of the lesser vehicles were buried alive, swallowed in ivy and brambles. You could read hieroglyphics into the misted curves of the windscreen. The officiating priest was a bronze Vauxhall with faux-American aspirations. It hummed. It buzzed in the traveller's fever dream.

He put his camera to the driver's window. There was a cat—still alive?—trapped on the passenger seat. Rubber, mud, slurry, rust, wet plastic: the beached boat of the car stank. It was Catling who put him on to Blackwood, on his first visit to the family den on Cobourg Road, back in the Sixties, when the author of *The Vorrh* was a sculpture student in Walthamstow. He showed the traveller his prize possession, the handsome 1912 edition of Poe's *The Raven* illustrated by Edmund Dulac. He showed him crime scene photographs of a transvestite suicide by hanging in Epping Forest. A gaunt junkie in his mother's black slip, lips painted, fatal rope counterbalanced with a breeze block. He said that the traveller should read *John Silence* and that other Blackwood story, "The Man Whom the Trees Loved". He showed disassembled rifles, bayonets, pistols, some reproduction, some auditioning as sculpture. He cooked a fierce curry and chilled it with yogurt. When he came outside to see the traveller off, still wearing carpet slippers, he trod in a fresh dog mess. He balanced on one leg, tumbled into a pratfall, and said from the pavement how much he admired Norman Wisdom.

The door of the Vauxhall was not locked. The black cat seethed and curled like crematorium smoke. Like a bonfire of monks' hair. One remarkable feature with the old soul that was Catling is how all the elements were in place from the start: the useful obsessions, the gift for self-invention, for shapeshifting and communicating with his elective affinities. He had a classic tale, out of Poe and much else, out of his own experiences, set in a pre-plague Liège (another border). There is a cat. And a girl with ice teeth. And a house contrived to fold in all the lurking horrors. The girl grooms the cat, in the way that monkeys do, tweezering fleas. Delicacies. That clicking sound is the splitting of the carapace, as the girl devours another succulent, fur-warmed morsel.

An inquisitive servant breaks into the set of rooms where an old man served the strange child. It is deserted. There is a smell he recognises in the "old part" of his brain. "It was the sweet cloying smell of meat and it was being massaged in the unventilated warmth of the apartment." The intruder, Pedric, imagines unholy couplings. He finds a bowl of rancid meat paste. He calls the cat by name. Lifting a sheet from the bed, he is confronted by a shadow in the curled shape of the missing girl. He reaches out to touch and the shadow spreads instantly over his hand, his wrist, the white of his arm. "They were fleas. Thousands of them. And now the ravenous infestation had a new donor to seethe upon."

The traveller slammed the car door. The cat broke into an angry vortex. He knew that his expedition was infested by creatures from other, more powerful stories. More potent renditions of the universal horror. The black cat was a furious mass of fleas, of maggots, replete, fed on shadows, waiting for a new host. The shadow was the essence of a departed cat with no shred of its original flesh left: no fur, claws, or teeth. Without Catling, the traveller would have left this well alone. What we choose to read is what we are obliged to see. Without preordained narratives we have no path to follow.

The muddy track laces into the fenced and shaved enclosure of the Shrewsbury Barrow. Without the Barrow it would not exist. It would have no meaning. The path flows in the same way that the underground water from the burst pipe runs down Burrage Road. The pregnant tumulus is a reservoir of untapped fictions. "Knives, arrowheads and bronze daggers would accompany the corpse," a notice informs visitors. Those instruments were already present in Steve Moore's suburban den. Now his ashes are among the fallen leaves. They are part of the smoothed roundness of an earthwork that is more like a marram-grassed sand dune than a place of interment. "If anything has been found inside it is not recorded."

What is notable here is the silence of these guardian avenues, the crescents baffling the irritation of sound from Shooters Hill in a complexity of labyrinthine choices. Hushed roads, where occupiers have dozed for centuries, run back into themselves. Aspirational estates built over a chain of other Bronze Age burials, markers of sacred contour lines, astral placements of the unsleeping dead along a ridge of vision above the serpentine river. Clusters of brazen tower blocks smother the print of primal mud villages invaded by electricity. Beech and elder: trees are witnesses. The traveller, running his fingers through a healing gash in the bark of a thick elephantine trunk, notes how the wound mimics the digressions of the younger Thames. And he recalls, without remembering the details, a story Steve Moore told on the one guided tour over this ground that the two men attempted. A car-jacker of the district, tyres screaming, made a furious circuit of these crescents. As if pursued by something worse than death. As if he wanted to deliver his stolen vehicle to the metal cemetery on Mayplace Lane. The car swerved, avoiding some lesser demon, a phantom from the Triassic era, and smashed into the tree alongside the Shrewsbury Barrow.

The trees of the avenue had seen so much. They shielded the traveller from watching eyes. They were the black widows, naked and proud, of an older and now forgotten way. Pavements are wide enough to walk. But nobody does. A lovely distillation of articulate light is trapped among threads of intermeshing branches. There is a vital communication beyond timid desire lines and messages from the universal grid. From Hartmann lines in a terrestrial magnetic field. The traveller's gradual ascent, sniffling, gasping for breath, has to accommodate the new horizontal rush, the temptation to lift into vision. Geobiologists have registered fault anomalies: sick headaches, stomach cramps, trembling palsied hands. Anxiety is a localised condition. So many electromagnetic devices exploit the hilltop. There are remnants of semaphore systems from distant wars. There are photovoltaic scanners and carcinogenic phone boosts. There is the Eaglesfield Mast, a bristling and barnacled tower given temporary license by the security alert of the Olympic moment. With that unchallenged permission never rescinded. The traveller yields to the microclimate of justified paranoia by circling slowly, layer by layer, through the cataleptic crescents.

Earning his eventual release onto Shooters Hill Road, and relishing the absurdity of a pointy-roofed villa, very much like the house in which he grew up in Wales, pushed against the redbrick thrust of a disguised gothic revival water tower, the traveller recalls Catling's yarns, from the day when they walked here with Steve Moore. Yarns about his adopted family, his Surreyside uncles from the railway arches around Borough Market. Uncles in hauling, in cooperage. And the parties up here in one of the properties he tried to identify. Memory can't handle numbers. The traveller got the sound of the labouring cars, the presence, not yet exploited, of the woods on the other side of the road. Catling remembered low ceilings in a tidy front room, women in the kitchen: the drink, the sociability where all are equal. And the overlapping banter in which he played his stuttering adolescent part. He was bigger than the space allotted to him. Always. From the crib. The tenement.

He was chosen, like a child of myth, and not presented to biological parents. As he told it to Steve, he did the choosing. In a version of supermarket sweep, Cockney foundlings were laid out in their trays, to be examined by prospective future guardians. He liked what he saw. He drew Len and Lil in towards him and he was right. Shooters Hill was noise. Sometimes the uncles moved a few yards down the road to the Bull, that ghost of a coaching inn. Now, as I passed, admiring ornamental tiles, I noticed above an antique road sign the faded lettering of an old boast: SPIRITS / OF THE / FINEST / QUALITY.

Which was the Moore house in the Hillend cul-de-sac? Was it number seven? There were no ladders or blue plaques. Some of the properties had drive-in garages, but everybody parked on the street. Those garages could store evidence of obscure hobbies.

Across the road from Steve's "manhutch with its pagan icon huddle", as Alan Moore called it, was the intimidating hulk of the Memorial Hospital. Intimidating by placement and by reputation. A sanctioned site of refuge and repair. Much needed in this borough. And doubtless starved of funds. Alan, as ever, was sensitive to atmosphere. He knew that, in dodging the flow of traffic, snake-head stick raised like Moses, and wading into the woods, he was in danger of "allowing this to turn to a John Silence story, to a yarn where the intrepid house-on-haunted-hill investigator is reluctantly, predictably drawn in and made a witness to the awful outcome, to the vanishing".

Who vanishes first? Hill or man or sanity? Time abraded with gentle strokes. Travellers sweat blood and dream of coffee.

As I held back, waiting for a break in the traffic, it struck me that John Silence might have the status of a figure from *The Cabinet of Dr Caligari*. As much inmate as doctor. Or both at the same time. Held in a padded cell scribbling about another life. Which only lasts as long as the prisoner keeps writing. Blackwood knew that Silence had once been Dr. Stephan. Was he attached to the Memorial Hospital? *From Caligari to Hitler* was the title of Siegfried Kracauer's influential study. And from that suggested cultural link the inevitable electromagnetic waves ran down to Woolwich and Thamesmead and Eltham. And all those pockets of rage and seething blunt-force discontent. Before damage and crisis brought the figures on both sides of the argument, racists and resisters, uphill in ambulances to the hospital on the edge of the woods.

Tangled in text, we qualify as somnambulists. We know that Caligari, the fairground mesmerist directing a series of murders by a dreamer kept in a coffin, is also the director of an asylum. "John Silence" was a convenient mask through which Blackwood could make his pitch and identify an acceptable readership for fantastic tales. Silence might have been, as depicted, a charitable man of independent means. He might also, in the wilder fiction we call life, have been controller of a private hospital very close to the grand house in which Blackwood was born.

How they babble! How they tune themselves to voices in the aether! How the walls talk! And what stories they tell! Silence says that if he accepted all the claims of clairvoyance from his patients, "statistics of suicide and lunacy would be considerably higher than they are". He knows that sinister "mind-forces" use unsuspecting brains for the dissemination of those monstrous lies known as novels.

At the opening of the path leading to Blackwood's first home, there is an advertising board with a pale painting, something approximating to the era of Ravilious and Bawden, in subdued, weather-bleached colour. A revised and romanticised version of the Blackwood property stands alone and proud in an English field. You can barely make it out now, but there is a sponsor's message hidden in the clouds: THE BEST KEPT SECRET.

"How long have things been coming apart in this way?"

Does he mean how long have I been out of sorts, thought the traveller? Or how long have I been losing it altogether when I step out in this direction? Nature or nurture. Prognosis or prediction.

"Do you think all the disparate and warring pieces can be fitted together, naturally or by medication, simply by relocating? Fitted to a single coherent construct? In other words, if you follow the logic of a story, without interference, is that story valid? Does it stand up?"

Before he could scan the chalked menu and take a punt on a cup of restorative hot chocolate, the traveller realised that it was not always about himself. The man with the wild eyes of Wittgenstein and electrocuted hair from *Eraserhead*, in a striped butcher's apron, safely behind the counter, was not addressing his potential customer. He was not addressing anyone. Perhaps he was rehearsing a play?

"Physician heal thyself. You have the run of the pharmacy. Anybody put in charge of a hospital of referred madfolk, with a belief in his own omniscience, must be crazy. Does that explain it?"

While the man talked, a black-haired woman with a smile for all seasons got briskly on with the business of filling a mug with sweet chocolate shavings and hissing steam. The traveller declined the offer of flakes, at no extra charge, and picked his way through the busy tables to an unoccupied slot right by the door. He was happy to find himself, once again, under that vintage poster for *La Dolce Vita*. And the monochrome print of Wood Lodge, where "in 1869 the writer, lumberjack, mountain climber, occultist and spy Algernon Blackwood was born". A subsequent owner, Sir Hay Donaldson, went down with Lord Kitchener when *HMS Hampshire* struck a mine on her way to Russia. "By the 1920s the former Blackwood house was derelict. It was demolished in 1932."

And yet here we perch, this interesting crowd, said the traveller. In a more ambitious building erected on the selfsame ground. On the border between established woodland and one clear and wide sweep of native grass. On a generous deck that feels like the balcony of England. Coast-bound traffic, it has to be admitted, still hums towards the rumour of Europe. The Rochester Way Relief Road, hidden by trees, links with the A2 and the orbital motorway. Seated figures in the steaming café, intent as Cézanne's card players, contemplate cheese sandwiches, their dogs restless on the floor.

With that first step on the path through the woods, in the general direction of what you hope will be the Oxleas Café—*is it still there, was it ever there?*—unconsummated legends of Shooters Hill are annulled. Yellow snapshots in a plastic wallet. The trees are primed for those who are willing to be absorbed, to donate their sap, to put down roots. There are waistcoats of ivy waiting to comfort or to choke. The walk from the road, around the painting of the Blackwood property, with its promise of secrets hidden in the passing clouds, recalibrates time. To find the café still active, bodies behind misted windows, is confirmation that we are welcome to repeat old mistakes, to return to those memories that were never our own.

Justified in some small way by the dimly reproduced photograph of Wood Lodge on the wall, but timid as yet of looking at it too closely, the traveller made a preliminary pass at his fellow recreationalists. Taking it from an actuarial or social science viewpoint, the table occupants, in their threes, fours, and sixes (animals and children included), divided into two general categories and several sub-divisions.

There were resting or preparing walkers, hikers with sensible boots and laminated guides around the neck. They were eager to accomplish the Green Chain circuit: anoraks, woolly hats, and Nordic ski poles. There were the inevitable canine buddies of the neighbourhood equipped with sodden grey tennis balls, gnawed to bare rubber, and devices for throwing them. You could characterise both these classes as loosely tourist, excursionist. Retired folk, with pensions, still on the right side of the grass, enjoying a well-earned interval of casual chat in a warm dry room. A number of them, mainly men, shuffled out to avail themselves of the facilities.

Then there were the disciples of Silence, elective mutes in painful proximity with fellow patients, incontinent babblers and shouters. The certified Trappists kept their heads down, turning no pages of the leaflets they hugged. The ranters hoped that their whitecoated judges would fail to recognise that an unbroken and unconnected monologue was silence in disguise. A smokescreen masking incorruptible affliction. Outpatients, on release from the house in the woods, parked their demons in the open air. Their clothes were not so different from those of the walkers. But it did not appear that they had chosen them. The clothes did not fit and they didn't go together to make an outfit, protection against the weather.

Solitaries all, they preferred to share a table, united in their special crust of solitude. One man was cutting up, in neat rectangles, ripped out sections of a paperback book. Which he then ate. With the fastidious disdain of a copyeditor. Another man, in the pretence that he was about to make a long distance phone call, licked semi-precious lapis lazuli stones, selected from a soup bowl. The traveller heard him yell: "I must purify the dialectic of the tribe." The lapidarist, overindulging, coughed and choked. He laughed. One of his companions smacked him on the back. A sharp stone had gone down the wrong way. A stern woman with spectacles dipped a spoon, her pinkie erect, into an empty saucer. Dabbing her lips with an inadequate paper napkin, bloody with drool, she snacked on air.

The silence in the photograph—it had to be measured now against these phantoms of the future carousing in vanished rooms—was absolute. The full-frontal aspect of Wood Lodge, shaped from three rounded two-storey turrets squeezed together, came back to life as the portrait of a man made from the particulars of place. Virginia creepers suggested the dark shadows of an overnight beard. Lichen violated a powdered façade. As he stood up to photograph the photograph, the framed copy of a copy of the original, the traveller saw his own outline in the glass, with the illuminated counter of the café behind him: Wood Lodge would be grafted forever across the dark outline of his chest. Three bushes on the lawn behaved like a posing family group, frozen in inherited dignity, when the house itself was the real subject. But they might have been a botanical arrangement or women disguised as young trees. Without wanting to invoke the obvious, by way of M . R. James, the traveller had to admit that a grey flaw in the grain of the print, spilling uphill across the open acres of the private garden, reaching towards the house and the trio of overdressed daughters, appeared to be growing, darkening, thrusting an arm or tentacle out ahead, as if to draw an invisible bow. The photograph was as unresolved as a set-aside Blackwood story.

Lips brown, a sugary rim of curdled froth from the last of the cooling chocolate, the traveller stepped outside. And was immediately overwhelmed. The empty tables bolted to their pedestals. The fixed benches, varnished struts glistening from fresh rain. He understood why this vision—and it was a vision, the lush slope waiting like the field at Battle for an invading army, pale hills under a leaden sky—was altogether too much for the café clients. Those inside held to their communal fug. And swirled the dregs in their dirty beakers. For the patently disturbed, in remission from urban anxiety, solitude was only bearable in the silence of the crowd. Which included the occasional bark or wolverine howl.

The former Blackwood estate, this verdant carpet, this public pleasure ground, this park, this England, was an invitation they declined. In shuddering terror. It spoke so seductively of a better way, another life. Everything was permitted until the unwary reached the preliminary line of the trees. Even the Green Chain walkers hesitated, before striking off, calling the dogs, identifying the approved path. The steady procession of males scuttling, tight legged, around the side of the café building, in the direction of what had once been the Blackwood greenhouses, for winter cultivation of soft fruits, were frustrated. The gentlemen's toilet had been secured, pints of hot sweet tea now regretted, metal roller blinds pulled down over the thick wooden door. OUT OF USE: PLEASE ASK FOR DISABLED KEY. But they would not, they were London proud, they were able. So there was another green chain, as the traveller observed, of elderly men rushing away from the house and into the Hanging Woods. The categories of café patrons divided again: veteran walkers to find a good tree behind which to relieve themselves and trusted inmates to identify and endure their tragic paths. To complete a circuit that would carry them safely back to the place from which they had come.

Innocence had fled. The traveller could not forget the sight to which Steve Moore had led him on that single memorable but almost forgotten walk. It was the season of the great global circus when our city abandoned itself to corporate colonisation, to war rules, heightened security delivered at whatever it cost. Through what was once a playground on the edge of the woods, a crop of lethal, swaying, anti-aircraft rockets had been sewn. Like the covert weaponry of Russians preparing to defend themselves against malign propaganda from Ukraine by demolishing residential blocks, power plants, hospitals, and schools. The Oxleas rockets were ready to go, independent of visible human operators. They were all over the fortunate Olympic boroughs and down the length of the Estuary. In public parks and on the roofs of occupied blocks of low-rent flats. The reality of this imposition could never be expunged. It was as Cormac McCarthy wrote about those gaunt and terrible hospitals into which ordinary people sometimes vanish. "After so many years even the bricks are poisoned. There are remedies but there is no remedy. Sites that have been host to extraordinary suffering will eventually be either burned to the ground or turned into temples."

That day with Steve, in the face of the challenge of this glorious expanse, did come back. Catling had been there too! When he was contemplating some way of taking the handbrake off and letting rip with a torrent of prose. Unsure how to give it form, he asked for advice.

The traveller bagged up a copy of *Blood Meridian*. Those little Victorian plot summaries at the section heads did it for the poet. "Now I get it," Catling emailed. Before attempting nothing of the sort. The waiting madness was far too rich and strange for any mere device. It would come like a fever and write him into another place. And through that place, he would become another person. Crows at the window would be substituted by the witness of angels.

The three men, unlikely companions, met by arrangement on Wellington Street in Woolwich, close to the Royal Artillery Barracks, where, a year or so later, Fusilier Lee Rigby, returning from duty at the Tower of London, was run down by a Vauxhall Tigra and hacked to death by two assailants with a simplistic and brutal world vision. Life had battered them to the point where they would have to slash it into ribbons and glory in madness. Shots were exchanged. The two Nigerians were Muslim converts. They attempted a beheading. One of the men, Michael Adebolayo, gave a video interview to a passing stranger, who was also presented with a handwritten justification. A police cordon was set up. The two men made a headlong charge with upraised cleaver and revolver. They were shot, taken to hospital, and later found themselves incarcerated in Belmarsh High Security Prison, in an industrial estate between Woolwich and Thamesmead. Both assailants had taken courses at the University of Greenwich, which was then situated in Woolwich.

Solutions invent problems. None of this had happened when the three writers met at the bottom of the hill. But it was there, present, implied in the temporary enclosures of the Olympic hallucination. The crackle of gunfire behind canvas screens, the ever-alert security. University, barracks, hospital, prison, parkland: all connected. The politics of deprivation and discontent. Eltham. Thamesmead. Factions. Criminal associations. Certain pubs on recovered marshland that did not welcome outsiders. Certain bookshops with backrooms of political pornography, where a man in a bad suit was always sitting in company with others, offenders who had never finished a book in their lives. Police and men of violence in comfortable agreement. Import/export down the river. Caravans on Sheppey.

Steve Moore, in his room at the top of Shooters Hill, didn't own a shooter. His weapon was a Samurai sword. Catling loved guns and their mechanisms with a Texan relish: as an article of faith, a set of sculptural possibilities. He was a maker, his dreams carried him down the Ridgeway to Waylands Smithy. These men had come together, all three, in the wake of Alan Moore's epic archaeology, his "Unearthing". Steve was embedded in that text, his future preordained. He believed in, and already occupied, an imaginative afterlife. But the traveller was not convinced that the author of *Somnium* believed in this one, contemporary interventions in an ancient landscape. Moore had the silvery aspect of a sage, a being who should never have been exposed to the open ground of Gun Park and Woolwich Common, to the deadly ballet of the rockets at the edge of Oxleas Wood. The crown of hair, bleached white by nights of study under a bare bulb, the black shirt, the slow and steady movements: these were the trappings of an oriental scholar. The English teeth were the reality. Steve attended to *The Book of Changes*, preferring to call it *Yijing*, rather than *I Ching*. He was less interested in predicting the future than becoming familiar with daily routine and ritual. The future wrote itself. It had already happened.

The traveller moved a little ahead as the strange trio, impossibly tangled in their discrete stories, began their assent of Woolwich Common, before turning east to Shooters Hill. Steve brandished his wand of a stick. Catling, in a heavy leather Gestapo coat, felt all of that weight. They were already ghosts. They belonged here in a way that the traveller never would. Catling, as he laboured, pausing every few yards to recover breath, heard the music, the voices of the uncles. Moore needed to be back among his papers, his objects, before the world bombarded him with too much unrequired information. There was something cruel about the siting of the hospital at the crest of the hill. The halt and the lame were scattered across the nursery slopes, clutching at gateposts, clawing at hedges, crawling towards shelters where buses did not pause.

After a digression, slower than the Würm glaciation, through the crescents, to a pause that felt unbroken at the Bronze Age burial site, a pit stop, passing in a flash, at the Bull Inn, the three men convened in Steve's room. His brother Chris, a one-eyed cactus fancier, was gone. Catling would surely have relished a meeting, a chance encounter with a Cyclops of the suburbs. One of his own.

Weapons were handled. Visions exchanged. But the crime had not yet been committed. Catling's magic was in the making. He had cast swords, where Steve acquired them. The big man blocked the window that looked down on the past of the river, the mud of origin. There was much to be accomplished before his characters could reach the estuary and give themselves up to the tide. It was a moment of melancholy without cause or consequence.

"Maybe there's a word to designate the opposite of mourning, what we feel not after someone dies but after they reappear," Alejandro Zambra wrote. These two men, the traveller considered, heavy with words and wisdom, were barely here. Here in words. They had reappeared without dying. Mourning is congenital. It doesn't abate. And it is always premature.

It was time now to step down from the deserted verandah, outside the café, and to make a trial of the woods. Some of the released patients carried rescued scraps of stale bread, sachets of salt tipped into their shoes, as a toll due to the forest. A safe passage through the trees demanded certain established rituals. Bread and salt. The silence of the woods was not the silence of the wards.

"Single dad found hanged in the woods," reported the *News Shopper*. "He was turned away from Oxleas just hours before." Garry Guest's sister is still looking for justice. The body of her brother was discovered by a walker. It was swinging from a tree. Mr. Guest had been refused a bed at Oxleas House, "due to space limitations". Where are we when sanctioned shelters can offer no shelter? Respite is provisional. Paperwork smothers action. Hospitals are overwhelmed. Some of those denied sanctuary took their own lives. Eighteen patients, having been returned from Oxleas NHS Foundation Trust to care in the community, committed murder. Management pressure—political pressure—is relentless. Favourable statistics must be achieved by institutions soliciting further funding. It is harder to be admitted to a specialist unit in Oxleas than to All Souls in Oxford. Those who are fit for treatment are deemed fit enough to be discharged. The circle closes. The unhoused take to the woods.

How should you walk these paths? The traveller stuck to the well-trodden way. He wasn't ready to follow the example of Beckett. Unwell in Dublin, where there were many madhouses but no psychiatrists, the young Irish writer endured London. His wanderings are recorded in poems and in the 1938 novel, *Murphy*. Had he experienced, as an interested visitor, one of the institutions favoured by Dr. Silence? Had Silence stood, in silence, at his shoulder, when he took note of discriminations of infirmity. "Melancholics, motionless and brooding, holding their heads or bellies according to type. Paranoids, feverishly covering sheets of paper with complaints against their treatment or verbatim reports of their inner voices."

"During the day, he trudged for hours on end around the streets and parks. He walked briskly: partly, he told his cousin, because he wanted to tire himself out so that he would sleep; partly because the regularity of the movement acted as a kind of anaesthetic, easing his troubles." So James Knowlson tells us in *Damned to Fame*, his Beckett biography. "He could cover as much as twenty miles a day."

He passed along and over these hills, that's sure. His Dublin friend, Geoffrey Thompson, facilitated access to the Bethlem Royal Hospital in Beckenham. Beckett made a number of research tours and put the material gathered to good use in *Murphy*. He was much taken with the way certain patients manifested absence. "There was no one there," he said with a trace of admiration. Copious notes were taken. Atmosphere absorbed. But Beckett was never a nurse. He did drive an ambulance, but that was in another country. He left the hard task of labouring anonymously among the wards to Wittgenstein.

"The Magdalen Mental Mercyseat lay a little way out of town, ideally situated in its own grounds."

Better to be on the tramp, twenty miles or more, out from World's End to Beckenham, and back, without a thought in the head, than standing at the fatal window, sitting at a desk confronted by memories, by books and spools of recordings. *What* did *he think about*? So many parks, cemeteries, names. Cresting another hill, another wave. Good to be back in the den, *never knew such silence*, the creaking of stiff shoes, boots abandoned, left in the road, on the steps of a church, unexplained. The earth might be uninhabited, nothing, not a sound, a dog breaking cover, snapping branches, leaving a smudged trail in the wet grass, not a sound.

Beckett had a method for dealing with forests. He admitted as much in *Molloy*. He read somewhere that any attempt to walk in a straight line, through a wood or into a trackless desert, results in the disorientated pilgrim describing a circle. The philosophical pedestrian must strike out on the loop, in the hope that it will lead him directly from launch point to destination. Some hope! The traveller can't remember the details. Or the outcome. But he borrows the thesis. Sticking to the shaded edge of the great sloping meadow that ran away from the balcony of Blackwood's former house, he follows the gentle sweep of woodland in the expectation of arriving back where he started. He carries no bread. He does piss against a gnarled oak and leave natural salt in his drying traces. Branches reach out to envelop him. To tap his pulse. Tear his coat. Rip a cheek.

"I did my best to go in a circle, hoping this way to go in a straight line." But this was not Molloy's country, not Beckett's either. There was none of the romance of undifferentiated bog between hill and sea. No fires in the gorse. None of those white roads between stone fields where strangers approach over miles. Without, at the point of collision, exchanging a single word.

The traveller plodded on, feeling the pull of the inner forest, the hope of losing himself without abandoning the clarity of a meadow swept of its demons. There was no temptation to look back. He was caught by peripheral vision: a tree, freed from the wider forest, had been domesticated on the tamed carpet, the grounds of the Blackwood villa. A sessile oak perhaps? He was no arboriculturalist and he didn't have a convenient reference book. The tree was a gallery of images, mementoes nailed to the bark, happy days recalled, beribboned in memorial tribute. These are old instincts. No use to the departed. But a valuable rite of passage for those who remain. Polished shoes treated with respect and left in place by the usual predators, animal and human. Un-nested by squirrels.

The fatality occurred, as the traveller discovered when he read the graphic library of the tree, on the 11th June in 2022. Steve Moore's birthday, eight years after death, after those posthumous sightings, coins cast, predictions made and fulfilled, heavenly alignments calculated. And the traveller's own. An anniversary to be feared as much as celebrated. Carl Donnelly, a well-presented young man of the district, trimmed hair and modest rim of beard, "lost his battle with mental health in Oxleas Wood". Tattoos. T-shirt. Cocktail glass raised. Unforced smile. There was a service at the chosen tree. Family and friends make regular returns. The merely curious pause and contemplate. Cellophane flowers are heaped around the base. With cups, candleholders, and floral lettering: BROTHER. SON. A partial biography in images: the beach, the lads, girlfriend, child on shoulder, a flat-faced dog. "Officers were called to reports of an unresponsive man on Saturday morning . . . His death is being treated as non-suspicious." Carl Donnelly was twenty-four years old.

A plaque with careful calligraphy and a border of tiny paw prints is partly screened by a pair of unnaturally white roses and a scatter of brown oak leaves speckled with soot. "A Soul Forgotten", it reads. And will continue to read until a night's wind brings back the missing words. There is also a blind putto, a baby angel with vestigial wings and the name CARLOS in black paint. SARAH has been added down the length of a chubby forearm.

The traveller returned to the café with its deserted deck. The man at the counter was still talking to himself. The woman was still polishing her silver spouts and scouring dirty cups. The menu was as vast and improbable as before.

The hikers and the dog folk had disassembled, as if in obedience to the whistle of a guide. The outpatients, rising as one, were taking their allotted exercise, going through permitted paths in the woods. In company. Alone. In silence. Content.

Would the gentleman take a bowl of blue stones, the comedian wanted to know, or a thick slice of book? Beyond obvious pain, the going down and the eventual expulsion, this random geological scoop was too much ballast. The traveller had no intention of being weighted to this place. If the day had taught him anything, it was that the dead are light on their feet. They don't need ladders. They can be netted for a while in words. Like the shadow of a passing crow across a sheet of laundry in a Hackney garden.

The pages delivered on a souvenir plate from Portugal were quartered, fork provided. Brown sauce optional. The cattle cake of paper pulp might have been chosen for its cover illustration, a grey-blue section of imaginary forest. "Rection", the traveller read. Before he risked the first bite. "Hard rection." The counterman was laughing at his own joke. Now even the walking spooks were gone.

"I thought you'd appreciate the Wittgenstein reference. Sadly, there is no truth in the myth that he did his time as an orderly in our local nuthatch. Under Dr. Stephan. He was upstream at Guy's."

Picture the romance of those lost years, lost to us. A great philosopher in doubt, submerged, somewhere in a city he did not love. Picture the entitled colonial life of doctors in suburban retreats and private asylums. Many, as Beckett noted, were Scottish. If it wasn't Canada or Ceylon, it was Beckenham, Bedlam. The counterman no longer resembled, in any way, the legendary Austrian. More like a drunken drill sergeant from Woolwich barracks, played by Freddie Jones or Ronnie Fraser, he rattled on, unscripted.

"What they do say is that Wittgenstein, between shifts, on nightwatch, at a loose end, fingernails chewed to the quick, availed himself of the doctors' private library. It suited his mood that there was nothing available but detective fiction, yellowbacks, pulps. Ernest Bramah, Austin Freeman, Sax Rohmer, Algernon Blackwood. He liked that name, Blackwood. It took his fancy. Probably sounded better in German. Blind detectives, dream detectives, psychical detectives. Medical men. Freeman was a consultant at Holloway Prison, you know, before he retired to a bomb-shelter of his own design, in his garden at Gravesend. He kept his own laboratory. And he also bound books. Solutions in these tales are achieved by essentially magical means. Dr. Silence was a fugue walker like Blackwood himself. Keep trudging on until revelation comes."

Two or three segments of the cut-up novel on the traveller's plate were enough to induce a reflex gagging, revulsion in the throat. Over-spiced sauce with the picture of an Oxford College didn't help. "The question has always been only, *how can I go on at all, not in what respect and in what condition*." It sounded familiar but it wasn't Beckett. It was a translation. "To be in England, while the Cone is being built in the Kobernausser forest, but to remain for all the future in England. What we do secretly, succeeds . . . What we publish is destroyed in the instant of publication. When we say what we are doing, it's destroyed."

"You've got it," the counterman said. "*Correction* by Thomas Bernhard. Hard to chew. Impossible to correct. Wittgenstein as architect of a Cone building at the heart of a blackwood forest."

To eat was not to absorb. To read was not to scour the tongue. The traveller's mouth was inky and dry. He took his plate to the door, so that he could scrape the macerated mess, unseen, into a bin.

At the end of the declining meadow, where path met trees, the Green Way had been made literal: the emerging procession, a crocodile in which each person, apart from the leader, who was sustained by communal pressure from behind, had a hand on the shoulder of the one in front. Like the gassed blind of the First War, eyes bandaged. Between hell and convalescence.

The performed madness which is our only protection against madness is the maddest act of all. It has such purity of intent.

When the traveller returned his plate, the counterman who had seen them all, the walkers, the image scavengers, and the ones who wanted to dowse for traces of Blackwood or Steve Moore, had his ultimate tag prepared, that shop-soiled and famously slippery proposition from *Tractatus* 7. 7. "*Wovon man nicht sprechen kann, darüber muss man schweigen.*" Anticipating, correctly, the traveller's wretched monoglot status, he provided his own gloss. "What we cannot speak of, we must consign to Silence."

The word is what there is. Dead or dying, our names are our meaning. And they will be soon forgotten, outliving us all.

HOUSE OF FLIES

"Those that at a distance resemble flies."

– J. L. Borges

The ones whose duty it is to clean up the site of a murder or a spectacular suicide, under commission from professional criminals, state investigators, or estate agents hellbent on disguising the stink of fate, say that despite fulfilling rigorous protocols, with vacuum pumps, high-pressure hoses, bleach and carbolic soap, the uninitiated always miss the coded confessions of those small sticky footprints along the buckled ridges of the cornice, across the smoked ceiling. Immortal flies have been paying their intimate respects to the freshly deceased, before lifeblood pools and congeals in the lower back. They perch and stomp, drinking from eyeballs tightening and shrinking into the skull. From gristled stubs of oyster in a shallow shell.

In the house of that legendary dealer, Nicholas Lane, among a nicotine-tanned autumn of uncatalogued books and papers, none of the nocturnal visitors, those excited, strung out, bibliophile addict collectors, with their cottonwool mouths and chapped white lips, their picked hangnails, nervous twitches, straining bladders, and their scratching sweating farting anticipation, noticed the state of the marital bed beneath its mulch of Uranian chapbooks, its locked room mysteries, French decadence, and precious samizdat pamphlets from *The Forgotten Shelf.* The decomposing outline of a recently removed cadaver had burnt into the horsehair mattress like a body negative recovered from volcanic ash.

The peeling black door with its seven bolts was open to the street. They had been let inside. Lane's absence was the confirmation of his continuing presence in other dimensions. They had only to wait. For days, weeks, years if necessary. The house becomes the man. The man disappears. He relocates: another city, a better death. Flies have absorbed the dealer's essence. They hide and dream. They wait for dark. For older gods to stir once more.

Huddled, in their mildewed black overcoats, around the draped Whitechapel bed, as they once stood, white-knuckled, elbows sharply angled, paws clenched, in whispered and amicable rivalry, at the Saturday stalls on Farringdon Road, waiting patiently for the sudden whipping away of the tarpaulin and the bestial, grabbing clawing punching scrum, they fingered the sacred Nicholas Lane catalogue scrolls from a lost world. From somewhere as remote and improbable as 1981. Sheets of wafer-thin yellow and rose paper flaked in their hands. Rusty staples punctured skin. They browsed, in sensuous reverie, delighted to know that all these items, these prices, belonged in an unreachable past. Fortunate owners, the ones who had actually received the gems for which they had paid in advance, were dead. Forgotten. Their libraries broken and scattered among perverse and solitary rooms across obscure districts in London's outer fringes, in damp Welsh cottages reeking of woodsmoke, patchouli and foxes, in narrowboats, in barns, ruined castles, decommissioned cinemas and active asylums.

Doyle, Arthur Conan, and Others. Strange Secrets, *Chatto & Windus, 1889. 1st ed. 32pp adverts at rear* dated April 1889. Cobalt blue pict cloth, blocked in black, silver and brown, spine gilt. An anthology of sensational fiction, supernatural and criminous, including "The Secret of Goresthorpe Grange". Spine faded and dull, gilt titling flaking, some sl foxing, else a very good, tight, fresh copy. Scarce. £ 60.00

Ford, D. M. The Devil's Peepshow. *Hurst & Blackett, 1907. Occult fantasy published anonymously by the author of "A Time of Terror". The Count and Countess Cagliostro appear in modern times and attempt to seduce power from the politicians of Britain. Not listed by Bleiler. Spine a little bumped else vg copy. Scarce.* £12.50

Machen, Arthur. The Hill of Dreams. *Grant Richards, 1907. Some damp-spotting, cheap paper browned. Frontis by Sidney Sime. Spine sl faded. VG copy.* £13.50

Lane, an M. P. Shiel disciple and major collector, made it his business to cultivate a barrister in chambers at Gray's Inn, teasing him with Aleister Crowley material knocked back by Jimmy Page, in order to absorb the collegiate atmosphere, and to walk at night, with the Satanic lawyer, through the silent squares and locked gardens. And to listen to tales of Shiel and Machen and A. E. Waite. Later, ankles broken, propelled on his crutch like Blind Pew, Lane travelled out to Amersham to see if any traces of the elderly Machen could be found; any inscribed books, manuscripts or letters left among friends and surviving ancestors. The failure of that quest, as so often before, only opened up other opportunities. A freshly arrived case of pristine Hogarth Press pamphlets and limited editions in Penn.

The juvenile ownership signature of Graham Greene on an English first of Céline's *Journey to the End of the Night* in an African missionary shop in Berkhampstead, where Greene had been schooled and where his father was the headmaster.

What had Shiel written about his fondly recalled residence in the oasis of Gray's Inn, his friendship with Machen? "We lived in an island in the sea of London, rather touched with enchantment, and the tender grace of that day that is dead and will never come back to me."

Fiddling compulsively with a gaoler's bunch of keys that swung from the greasy tie he wore as a belt around the swag of his belly, keys for which nobody could assign a lock, one of the collectors began to tremble as he identified, in the second Lane catalogue, an obvious sweetener for the tame barrister. A man who was, at that time, embroiled in a complicated but generously remunerated defence of a breezy City fraudster and fellow Mason.

> *Machen, Arthur.* Hieroglyphics. *Grant Richards, 1902. 1st ed. Cloth a little soiled and chafed at edges, paper spine label rubbed. Good-vg. Aleister Crowley's copy with his firm pencilled signature on ffep. £28.00*

Drawn by these terse but magnetic descriptions into an occulted sense of actually *handling* the items they strained to picture, caressing the weave of the paper, the absorbed drops of Crowley's cold sweat, his toxic DNA, they were made aware that all traces of natural light had been withdrawn from the dealer's Whitechapel cave. Surely somebody in this deserted house had stolen in on them, on padded feet, a spectral retainer from the candle-lit depths of a subterranean, stone-flagged kitchen? An invisible hand sliding down the heavy oilskin blinds?

And securing their blasphemous transgressions from the witness of ordinary passing immigrants, respectably established with grocery shops, racks of wedding saris, ritual butchery, mini cabs. But there were no blinds. No servants. No visible ghosts. The windowpanes were blackened by seething layers of flies, feeding on the last glints of stolen sunlight.

The flies. The punctuation in the catalogues. The black tobacco spots and carcinogenic lumps on the necks of that coven of frustrated collectors. They were all part of the same alphabet. All fading, dying, making one last punt at cracking the great mystery of existence.

In his Dynevor Road retreat, not quite five miles from the House of Flies, Simon Toate, an alienated incomer, a mere twenty or so years in Stoke Newington, held his ground, swaying a little as he became accustomed to the pitch and roll of successive waves of influence, memories that were not his own. Through his willed divorce from everything that was familiar—childhood, school, another England— and the expulsion to an address endured by Joseph Conrad in his seafaring days, Toate had earned the freedom to doctor an unexceptional CV. Estranged from all that had come before his arrival in a north Hackney satellite famous for its proud sense of locality, its artisan stores and ethical cafés, the pirate podcaster burnished a reinvented self by compulsively trawling digital archives, attending agitated gatherings in the upper rooms of public houses, and misidentifying sites with dubious literary associations. He paid his respects to reputations mercifully rinsed in the euthanasia of neglect by slashing through resistant jungles of non-conforming Abney Park memorials, in order to phone-capture graves suitable for broadcast to the faithful few.

On this once-in-a-lifetime September morning, the lines of force were running like shoals of mackerel, swooping through shallows, chasing and chased, offering themselves to the scoops and buckets of amateur fisherfolk. Everything outside the window was new. Novelty was dredged from those currents of a past deemed worthy of resurrection and improvement. *Toate did not dare to move.* He might never move again. He held his breath until his aura expanded to fill the chamber. The covert aspect of Dynevor Road was absolute. And satisfactory. Here was a suburb of suburbs, tidy and self-contained, more sympathetic to the Victorian cemetery with the Egyptian gates than to the High Street and the road out. Dynevor Road was a closed system. It looped back on itself in a circuit of dim complacency that required no exit.

The worked-over draft for the next spontaneous podcast, to be delivered in panting excitement, as if by a man on the run, rushing to cover the ground within limits of a deadline set by no one but himself, fretted untouched on a damask-draped table. "Righteous Women Wronged", the yellow prompt-pad boasted. "We reveal a sisterhood of priestess poets patronised or diminished by that masculine inability to read with due care and attention. The males in discredited early-20th-century fictions smoke and stroll. They dine and drink and whore. They dabble in Golden Dawn rituals. They don't have proper jobs or households to run. They make leisurely expeditions. They have private incomes or clerical occupations that can always be set aside. They walk. Active women are entombed behind the curtains of airless rooms."

The pitch was dull and Toate was not the person to make it. He, more than most, was the very thing he feinted to denounce. The fat black period with which he always anchored his script, after the original inspiration stalled, seemed to be getting bigger. And blacker. An inky boulder against further progress. Did the feeble thesis he was formulating stand up? And, if not, could he make it palatable with a top-dressing of chappish banter? Get your cynicism in first. Toate, despite his Stoke Newington credentials, was not so much woke as undead: a zombie sleepwalking through the dreams of strangers, the stories of Poe and Stevenson and Machen. But he had a map. Touching it, tracing projected routes with a stubby finger, he linked the women, his poets, to known addresses. Then linked those addresses to the notion of a chain of interconnected cells, humming with pain and purpose. Conceptually hauling in the rope, from the one fixed point in Dynevor Road, his own timid consciousness, revealed a culverted stream, a previously unrecorded dance of active particles in perpetual transit from the shared burial pit of Catherine, wife and collaborator of William Blake, in Bunhill Fields, to the modest resting place of Emily Gosse, wife and mother, in the thickets of Abney Park. These lines were tendrils, roots, threads: urgent and untapped. They hummed with photochemical telegrams.

Like blind crows disputing a stale crust flung from a speeding vehicle, these hermits in their sour dens kept their discoveries close as a rabbit-skin vest sewn on a winter orphan. They were the last vestiges of the Stoke Newington brotherhood of the panelled bar, of smoking rooms in which no one was permitted to smoke. Toate had mentioned one of the dead poets to Stewart Lee, a luminary of the district who spent much of his life staying well away, on tragic English roads. A poet of particulars himself, Lee was the acknowledged laureate of the foil tray and the Premier Inn. Now chortling in merry complicity, the neighbours plotted to penetrate the secure, high-walled burial ground between Balls Pond Road and the Overground railway. Meanwhile, they hunted for rare books on sites they kept to themselves, in the hope of acquiring some remarkable and unique item of trade that might secure for one of them—*but only one*—a prized invitation to the House of Flies.

Post-mortem, the women sang like mermaids, but not to Toate. They laid down a sugar trail that he could dowse but never understand. His methods were crude: he followed his nose and headed for home. He navigated, like an ancient mariner, by the frost of his beard, trusting the salty bite in his sweat. Pitfield Street drifted into Whitmore Road and he got across the canal. The first confirmation of madness came as he approached fashionable De Beauvoir Square. A plaque on Mortimer Road advertised the cruel omission of Emily Gosse (*née* Bowes). Husband and son are recorded with their dates, a boasted legend of occupation. Emily, lyricist and author of numerous tracts, is unregistered. She was a valued sister among the Plymouth Brethren, dutiful and suppressed. Her accepted wrongs were expressed in horrid assaults from alien growths. The rack of torture bringing her closer to a pure white dress, a path walked barefoot with the Lamb. Toate chokes on the hurt he feels this woman endured, submitting to her imprisonment, her co-habitation with public men, the cranky scientist and the established author.

In an over-stimulated state, willing the assault of signs, the podcaster hurtles on, swerving and swearing through the traffic of Balls Pond Road and into Kingsbury Road. Taking his lead from Machen, Toate blundered into the same category of fabulous and inevitable discoveries. The kind that only exist on paper.

There was that "Strange Occurrence in Clerkenwell", when the immediate locality of a clerical drudge becomes "the cabinet of his studies". Strategic wandering releases pressure. Pressed knuckles against tired eyes reveal glittering galaxies.

"Dyson saw at once that by a succession of hazards he had unawares hit upon the scent of some desperate conspiracy, wavering as the track of a loathsome snake in and out of the highways and byways of the London cosmos; the truth was instantly pictured before him, and he divined that all unconscious and unheeding he had been privileged to see the shadows of hidden forms, chasing and hurrying, and grasping and vanishing across the bright curtain of common life."

The scent of violets drowned in milkbottles, that was it! From the Kingsbury Road burial ground, padlocked against *escape* and not intrusion, came a subtle earthy ripeness. Tropical rubber leaves dripped with pearly globules. Untramped grasses devoured the stone. A handsome red-gold vixen sprawled on the lid of a lichen-pillowed monument. There were drop curtains of ivy and an intricate cobweb doily exposing a larder of desiccated flies to the corona of the setting sun. Pressing his lardy face hard against the bars of the iron gate, left deep white stripes that did not fade until Toate caught his reflection in the mirror of the rented bedroom. In that instant, he knew what was disturbing him and what made a further expedition to this site essential: the enclosed garden of remembrance for the nameless Jewish dead was green and fertile and damp with ancient shadows, while the rest of London was burnt and shrivelled and parched from long months without a drop of rain.

Improvising wildly, gripping so hard that he almost snapped his pen, the podcaster attributed this meteorological anomaly to the rumoured presence, inside those brick walls, of the remarkable poet Amy Levy. Her challenging stare! Those unforgiving eyes! Awful self-knowledge. Slavic. Cap of tight dark hair. The formal portrait with high lace collar reminded Toate of a postcard he had found once in

Spitalfields, an orphaned Australian Aboriginal child. She had been taken in, dressed and churched by the governor and his wife. Abandoned, without a second glance, when they returned to England, the young woman died early and hard, from alcoholic poisoning.

Levy was a prisoner of solitary rooms in houses that were never her own. She made it her business to break away: Cambridge University, an intimate association with Vernon Lee in Florence, novels, stories published by Oscar Wilde. Then, before her thirtieth birthday, a profound and muffling deafness, the struggle to catch her own words, rhythms of an inner voice. And a single desperate inhalation of carbon monoxide. Death within doors. Death of the home. A room that was forever her own. Exposure and retreat: at a terrible cost. Poems laid out across virgin paper, where they could not be denied. She meditated on horrors beyond the cloudy glass of the bell jar: "He comes; I hear him up the street— / Bird of ill omen, flapping wide / The pinion of a printed sheet, / His hoarse note scares the eventide." Again and again the fated insinuation: that street, this city. The bird of augury. The raven. The tell-tale crow. It can only be assessed from a fixed position, as Toate knew. A borrowed room in a family house in a desolate suburb. The portal of a prison window. "Here from my garret-pane, I mark / The plane-tree bud and blow" or "All things I can endure, save one. / The bare, blank room where is no sun" or "The sad rain falls from Heaven, / A sad bird." Excitement beyond fixed bounds. The pains and pangs of movement and co-existence. More pain and pages inside.

Shipwrecked in his Dynevor Road attic, Toate recalled the route by which he started to trespass on the achievement of the poets, on the lectures and small press anthologies for which, at some future date, he would be rewarded.

Women at the Window: Three Reforgotten Hackney Poets.
With afterword by Chris McCabe of the National Poetry
Library. The secrets he might trade with Stewart Lee. The
rare books offered as a bribe for entry to the House of Flies.
Without taking a single step towards the window, Toate
reached for his pack of coloured pens. And drew a series
of wild, overlapping and tangled lines across his map. That
concluding period, the ink-bright full stop, was in fierce
relief. It stood alone and proud, meniscus swollen to a
dome-like curvature.

Unplaced, in the way that Machen sometimes
found himself on the boundaries of Bloomsbury and
Clerkenwell, pulled east and west by equal forces, Toate
mislaid the invisible thread that had dragged him through
the labyrinth of unknowing that is Outer Hackney, a
slumbering and mysterious zone of dead ends and satellite
suburbs forever doubling back on themselves, teasing
the unsuspecting tourist towards the souks of Kingsland
High Street and Stoke Newington Road. So it was that
the podcaster summoned up his persistent and illegitimate
fantasy: a woman wearing a man's V-necked charcoal
sweater in the upper room of a corner house on Amhurst
Road. The prolific and delirious poet, Anna Mendelssohn,
took flight in the guise of many projections, including the
Cambridge shed-dweller, Grace Lake. She was closest to
Toate in time, a near contemporary. More than any of the
others, she resented his impertinent intrusion. "I . . . am
not good at / being immobile", Mendelssohn wrote. That
room, those walls! "Walking is to make poetry / poetry
is emptying the page and filling / in space in continuous
motion / of breath / Breath is paradise."

Toate pressed the balsa bones of his avian chest. The page
on the table in Dynevor Road was smudged. His shoulders
shook like those of a guilty man hoping to avoid the insult

of a full body search. He was a supplicant postponing X-ray diagnosis by tugging down an inadequate string vest. If the page emptied, it was because there had never been anything there. Mendelssohn with the rubber letters of her John Bull printing set kept the demands of her art ahead of slogans and warnings. "A full stop," she remembered, "was what I was working for." Unhappily, she concluded, "my mind was not in my feet." On the far side of the ceaseless main road, uniformed mercenaries bundled handcuffed and protesting suspects into a notorious police barracks, set back from casual pedestrianism, and protected by the sinister dullness of its uncivil architecture.

As Toate's rogue full stop *moved* of its own volition, threatening to bring down the entire design by making the virgin white-field black, he shot out a fist and squashed the bug. The fly. The malarial messenger. He felt the tickle of diaphanous and folded wings. Blood, involuntarily donated, squirted over the postcard he used for a bookmark. Blake's visitation, "The Ghost of a Flea", made literal. He would send it to Stewart Lee and suggest a walk.

They picked the wrong night. After leaving her keys on the table and the front door wide open to all comers for the last time, the in-occupation wife of Nicholas Lane flattened the spread of newspaper with scabbed elbows, before composting the surface with a layer of thick black treacle. In the heart of working Whitechapel the heat had been unbearable. Buckets of chickens' feet seethed with maggots. When Lane was in residence, the timeless Georgian house cultivated shadows. Candles flickered. Grotesque shapes—book towers, guitars, Polynesian masks scavenged from Cheshire Street—played their cinematic phantoms, like Nosferatu or Caligari, across walls and secret shelves draped with sheets. Sleep was impossible:

Satan's flies droned, swooped, fed. Every morning a fresh topography of angry wheals, recalibrating the map of skin, prophesied alternate futures. Red bumps improved the badly inked designs, Taoist and nautical, blood-needled into ankle and exposed shoulder. Hieroglyphs struggled to tell the same tale, to sound the same warnings: a Rosetta stone of dead languages on unpeeled living parchment. The dust of centuries danced to unheard melodies, to the Delta blues guitar that Lane lacked the hours to service. The dealer's touch was shamanic. He drew in persons of consequence. Books, objects, insects, unbidden, filled his sack. The only rumour of rain in many parched months, when stepping outside, was madness. It came from the hiss of phantom sewing machines in garret and cellar, from all the narrow tenements overlooking the unstoppable passage of a buried river.

Flies moved between the lines with darting tongues. Flies remembered séances, the teasing of William Blake. Flies made new words from their copulations and lifted off to erase them. Flies paddled in the slurry of treacle, the oily quicksand, and were caught.

Stewart Lee, a trained student with a quick eye, reminded Toate of an episode that John Gawsworth reported, when the newly married Machen, who enjoyed accompanying his wife to the theatre, returned home to find the corpses of 120 flies massacred across a jammy newspaper trap. Mrs. Machen was triumphant. The articles Arthur struggled to complete were orchestrated by the hysterical buzzing of 3,000 flying, circling, unkillable demons. He couldn't know that his great-granddaughter, Tessa Farmer, with his own copies of the books he had written secure on her shelf, would contrive her magical art from the belief systems of these alien others. There was a karma of slaughter in that hot summer room to be recognised and appeased. Farmer, Oxford schooled like Lee, in necessary disciplines—taxidermy, anatomy, cosmology—said that she considered herself an "intermediary" rather than an "artist". Her fairies were harbingers of death, themselves trapped in tensile webs strung across windows, in the shrubs of collegiate gardens. They accepted the contract of mortality, generations passing and renewing in a blink. Walking in the wake of the older women poets, losing herself in the same streets which were never the same, the Oxford artist carried tweezered corpses back to the high room where she could scalpel miniature autopsies. Playing god, with the approval and encouragement of her mentor, Professor Catling, she rebirthed her newly minted creatures into fantastic scenarios. "I never kill," Farmer said. "I give house to dead things from the streets. It has been so hot this summer. I find so many wasps. It was a very strange but inspirational feeling to read my great-grandfather's books. His little people come out of the ground. My fairies are made of plant roots."

Questing book collectors can never, despite the best of bad intentions, go hunting together, when it comes to the kill. But how pleasant it was to recall conversations on pre-dawn drives out of the city, into Norfolk or Lincolnshire. Stories exchanged, rumours and gossip floated. Dealers return in warring silence, bags secure beneath tightly clamped knees. Toate knew and respected Lee as a Stoke Newington pundit, a person who read widely and shared his discoveries with the faithful. There was another life too as some kind of performer, but he paid no attention to that. It went with the Oxford pedigree. They were all performers, those boys, skilled at catching the mood of a crowd and playing it back: Bill Clinton and Howard Marks, Tony Blair and his tight-trousered tribute band. And those Bullingdon boors richly rewarded for confessing on game shows, lying without shame on the podium, and running the country as a hobby. But Toate had not expected the bicycle clips. Lee was a solid, confident figure, with the upraised eyebrows of a genial and liberal eighteenth-century magistrate. He had listened to all the crimes of the poor and their persecutors and now it was his turn to rave at iniquity, before passing sentence. He was a walker, a mountain walker perhaps, with a hooped spine aching from many hours driving up and down the country. That was how Lane got his start in the business, killing mornings in provincial towns before the other musicians in the van woke up. Those books by Shiel and Machen, by Djuna Barnes and Mina Loy, were waiting in Penzance and Preston, in Peterborough and St. Leonards-on-Sea.

The stoic comedian caught Toate's furtive lizardly glance.

"Habit," Lee said. "We all wore clips, back in the day. Especially for kids' matinees in Solihull. None of us had bikes, but as soon as we were into long trousers, we had a trick to keep the fleas out."

The two men met at Swedenborg's grave, on a druggies' bench under the peeling plane trees, and strolled, side by side, to the House of Flies. The baked allotment beds were strings of shrivelled plants. Lee, three days unshaven, hair abundantly *en brosse*, was in humour, amused by the world and the infinite possibilities hidden within the shifting dimensions of Lane's house. He had something to trade, a few frames of unviewable sixteen millimetre nitrate stock featuring Arthur Machen's impersonation of Dr. Johnson, shot in Gough Square in 1922, for a film called *The Romance of London and Londoners*. There were no recorded prints in archives anywhere. Lee had acquired this rarity from a character actor friend, when they met to discuss how the brief residence of genial Irish entertainer Val Doonican, in a Highbury house, might have influenced past and future inhabitants. An authentic Machenesque conceit, Toate conceded. But Lee did not, this time, want a book. He hoped to persuade Lane to part with the asthmatic cassette he'd cut in a Ménilmontant booth with a pick-up group, including fellow Paris exile Michael Moorcock. The band were known in their three-month prime as "Les Homewreckers". Only five copies of the original cassette got out, with Lane's artwork and holographic additions. Tracks included "Feeling Weird", "Nikki's Staring at the Walls", and a collage of chopped up lyrics from Machen's *London Adventure*, produced by razor blade and cocaine.

Toate's proposed swap for the House of Flies was simpler: a brown envelope of cashmoney in exchange for four of the unpublished pieces Machen contributed to ephemeral broadsheets far scarcer than *The Gentleman's Magazine*. It was reported by the funeral goers in the mildewed coats who gathered at night around the indented bed, waiting for the great pipe-legged scavenger to return with his black briefcase of treasures, that Nicholas Lane had triumphed. He had located three of the "horror tales" composed by Machen in "a kind of agony" for *The Unicorn*, a fugitive publication that collapsed before his anguished efforts could appear in print. Lane had paper proofs. Lacking the contemporary newspapers the dealer would never allow into the house, his wife had adopted those precious Machen pages for her flytrap. The regiment of gorged and dying muscidae collaborated on an artwork that would never be displayed by Tessa Farmer. They were hieroglyphs of confusion, untranslated testaments to a lost civilisation in a lost city.

Back on the pavement, among scurrying figures, those who had somewhere to be, and who were guided and controlled by their handheld devices and prayer beads, the disappointed bibliophiles let themselves be transported towards the legend of the long vanished Whitechapel mound. The peeling door, twenty-five yards north of the pit in which the Ratcliffe Highway murderer had been granted a vampire's burial, slammed shut behind them for the last time. Nothing stirred the heavy drapes. There would never be a living human presence in the house again. The cracked and filthy panes of the windows were sealed by renewed squadrons of warring flies.

Slouching, side-by-side, Lee's bicycle clips giving off the occasional spark as thick calves rubbed, the collectors made the best of dashed hopes by competitively pitching theories derived from their ill-disciplined binge reading during the latest lockdown. Comfortable conspiracies in place of active resistance. Occulted politics ahead of the natural magic of weeds between paving stones.

"Did you ever?" Lee hesitated. "Did you find that . . . visit that . . . actually get inside . . . Lane's shop? Gone now for sure."

"At the back of King's Cross? Saint Pancras?"

"Machen *hated* Saint Pancras. Gothic fraud drawing attention to itself. And the trains went to places in which he wasn't interested."

"Northdown Street? Collier Street? Or was that in one of the London books? That yarn is so far-fetched, it has to be true," Toate said. "With the open street door, any idiot could blunder into the House of Flies. Drug fiends. Rough sleepers. Yanks. Lane was never there and nothing was for sale. In the shop, everything had a pencilled price—and people still collect those. Lane would arrive in the middle of night, fresh from the Edinburgh train, drop a bag and disappear. Dealers camped out. Collectors saw new items through the shutters when they came back from getting a coffee or taking a dump in the station."

It was agreed, before they reached Vallance Road, that the only way forward was to go back to the start at 4 Verulam Buildings, Gray's Inn. And by retracing Machen's now fixed trajectory—words set, flies settled—recover a conclusion the Celtic magician was canny enough to hold back. Toate had his musings on the alignments of the fierce women poets and the roots and threads beneath the stones of London. Lee had a scholar's faith that, eventually, all the tales must come into alignment, and that one more pamphlet, one cassette recording found in a Dalston charity shop, in Stockholm or Stamford, would complete the cosmic jigsaw and bring about a golden dawn in which he would receive his overdue laurel crown, while the hideous tribes of corporate criminals with their political clowns and bagmen would be led off to the tumbrel.

"It's on. It's on. It's *happening* today," Toate shouted. "Definitely on. Definitely. I was waiting to get across Farringdon Road, right opposite Greville Street, because I wanted to check out Moorcock's Bleeding Heart Yard, and this grey van shot right at me, jumping the lights. And you know what was painted on the side? GRAYS INNS KITCHEN! A sign or what? Because *immediately* after that, when I changed my mind and came up those haunted stairs to Holborn Viaduct, with the silver dragons, red tongues extruded, staring down to where the bookstalls used to be, and the statue of the woman with a quill or a dart and a board with her curling map of everywhere we have to walk today, and all the domes of law courts and cathedrals like the humps of beached whales, I was completely disorientated. It was like Machen said, I mean beyond the point where you know *everything* and you have set your foot on every broken slab, and out of nowhere it's all gone. He confessed, as you appreciate, that he was 'utterly at a loss to know where he was, or what he was doing, without the faintest notion of the various positions of north and south, east and west'—and that was it, my situation, precisely. The sun was hidden in a mantle of cloud. It might have been extinguished. I was fumbling back east, under the dictation of those stone effigies and the terracotta masks of red-faced Green Men of the woods with full Alan Moore beards. I knew it was wrong but I kept walking, faster and faster, Old Bailey, then the awful prospect of the misappropriated Temple Bar: Machen wrote about that and about St. Paul's. One of his characters said that Temple Bar was his first memory of London and that he witnessed it being pulled down from its original position in Fleet Street, 'in the dead of night, all covered with scaffolding on which flares were burning, and it looked like a sacrifice to Time on a flaming altar'. And I spun on my heels, arms wide, and *ran* and found myself once again, like hitting a page with its corner turned down in a book to which you are returning after a long convalescence. And here I am, just as you walk through the open gate and onto the cobbles and up to the arched entry at number 4, Verulam Court. Amen."

Lee's eyebrows, always amused, rose in pantomimed alarm to duplicate the curvature of the arch with the keystone dated 1811. He understood what he was getting into, but he was game, ready for a day's walk with no obligation to compose a report or write a single word. The walk was already written, already walked, by himself, and by crocodiles of Machen enthusiasts who excavated every published instruction and came no closer to finding the floating gardens, Poe's boarding school, or the reason why confirming a route was the best way of securing its mysteries for another generation.

The tight-lipped smile of the improvisatory genius snuffed Toate's rambling monologue. The two men had stared long enough at reflections of swaying forests in the windows of the high brick collegiate frontage of Verulam Buildings. They had imagined that the wooded avenues had moved, to squat *inside* the comfortable apartments of lawyers and gentlemen of means. Perhaps Machen had faced the gardens and not the busy road? But access was denied to outsiders, for whom the gates did not open until midday.

Lee tapped his lips with an upraised finger. The content provider had done his homework, he had a passkey. A measure of cult fame has its advantages. There were old university contacts still in play. Complimentary tickets exchanged for legal favours, assistance with writs and contract disputes. The scruffy pilgrims slid, unchallenged, through a postern gate. Breathing hard, they found themselves in a place beyond the dreary permissions and discoveries of the street. The broad and shaded walks of raked gravel belonged elsewhere. Toate, at once, called up Versailles and the Ghosts of the Petit Trianon, the curtain of time parting for two educated English ladies in 1901. And how executed aristocrats from the eighteenth-century appeared to them, along with a person of vile aspect, wearing a sombrero hat. The figures here had spades and brooms. Young women on heels moved swiftly with their cooling coffee flasks.

As they came on Verulam buildings from the other side, pushing into the shrubbery, ducking under branches, the impression formed that they were starting from the wrong place, the place where it should have ended. Lee, the omnivorous reader, thought of Eliot. "As we grow older / The world becomes stranger, the pattern more complicated / Of dead and living. Not the intense moment / Isolated, with no before and after, / But a lifetime burning in every moment." He knew, for example, that Machen's quest for

Canon's Park did not belong in Stoke Newington, but in what the writer saw, in those months of despair and silence, from his window here. "Desire itself is movement." What happened was a winding outward of the thread, a deliberate misplacing to ameliorate the consequences of vision.

These Gray's Inn groves, a few yards deep, were a miracle of interwoven bucolic density obliterating all the noises of the city. Even the avenues, the grand walks, were no longer visible. "In deep dells, bowered by overhanging trees, there bloomed flowers such as only dreams can show." And five steps beyond the thicket, in a sunken area, two lawyers smoked and plotted and laughed.

"And that is London," said Lee. "Conspiracy and consequence."

The purity of the Machen story was already undone, they would continue. They had no choice. Beside the great studded door of the lodge was a section of wall where the stucco had peeled off to expose a map of decay that Toate photographed, before tracing its white ridges and powdered scars with trembling prehensile fingers.

On Gray's Inn Road they gave themselves up to the process of converting a series of fictions that Machen had contrived, at such a cost, from documented excursions into a shuddering reality. Toate, the podcast philosopher, yelped at the excitement of catching this wave. As Machen had been confused, submerged in misery and silence, struck down, trapped in his tobacco-fug chamber, so he struck out, always on foot, letting the ground dictate his direction of travel. He writhed, "literally sobbing in the hysteria of despair". And that, Toate asserted, was a necessary condition for summoning and shaping the parturition of a masterpiece. Machen ventured alone, or accompanied by Waite, but shadowed by imagined characters more real, more deeply embedded in the matter of London. Things happened. "Great gusts of incense" were blown into his nostrils. Odours of rare gums had him swooning. A curl of cigar smoke travelled impossible distances, from enclosed courts and Soho windows, from Clerkenwell and Bleeding Heart Yard. "For that day and for many days afterwards I was dissolved in bliss, into a sort of rapture of life which has no parallel."

So it was for Toate, the Stoke Newington adept, who had, as yet, written nothing. Machen was sensitised by loss—wife, empty pages—to a neurotic degree. He mortgaged his soul to the traffic of the town, the call of subterranean currents, unseen roots and rivers recorded in Australian Aboriginal sand paintings, before they blew away. Toate limped, he muttered. He dragged a blistered foot, while Lee, glistening slightly, favoured cool shadows from high walls and buildings shrouded and propped in scaffolding. Together, they negotiated numerous pedestrian diversions around abandoned holes. The genial comic fell-walked with Edwardian vigour. He was happy to be facing north, pulling back towards his unrevealed address.

"Socks," Lee admonished. "Your trainers are fine, but unless you get the right socks, its 'gall to your kibe', as Powys wrote, was it *Wolf Solent*, one of those big ones. The stitching gathers into a knot."

When they came to the patch of grass, before the Dental Hospital, Toate took the split lid of a tombstone as the excuse for a photograph and a breather. The neat fissure in the igneous stone was more like a torn skirt than the consequence of frantic legs kicking against restraint. The park, with its tilted monuments, its day-sleepers on hard benches and filthy bundles left to reserve a favoured spot for the night ahead, was a tempting rehearsal for the paradise garden for which they were searching.

Grasping Lee's resistant elbow, Toate piloted the famed comedian through an angry swarm of cabs and bicycles, in order to follow the direction to which the crack in the tombstone was pointing. On the west side of the road was Canolfan Cymry Llundain, a centre for migrant Welsh making good with their cows and dairies and television careers in the foreign capital. *There had to be a clue.* Civil servants and dental hygienists drifted inside to gossip over lunchtime sandwiches.

While Lee searched for someone on whom to try the few Welsh phrases he had picked up on his rambles through the Cambrian Mountains, Toate stood transfixed by the time-stopping arrangement of a certain armchair against bars of sunlight on a geometric floor, against an antique radiator and the diamond panels of the leaded windows. The empty chair, its back to the street, summoned the absence of Machen. No, not that. *It was Machen.* Attempting to sit in the great writer's place was impossible, an impertinence. Lee followed a Cockney odd job man downstairs to a locked library the size of a boot cupboard. There were stacked shelves of books of Welsh interest: historical, sporting, legendary, musical, theological, poetical. None of them were by or about Arthur Machen of Caerleon.

Beyond King's Cross, the pilgrims found no trace of Nicholas Lane's shop or the antiquarian enterprise in Collier Street mentioned by Machen. Dulled surroundings made the slight incline hideous to lungs and fading spirits. The ponds and wells of Pentonville revived them. It was like dipping burnt faces in green jelly. Upper Street in Islington was moderately alive, sustaining commerce and coffee, but not worth a notebook entry or any advance on the Machen project—which might have petered out entirely on Balls Pond Road, if Toate had not recovered his proposed desire line. And Lee had not noticed, in a basement area, parched plants giving off, at the death, the sour scent, cabbage and drains, of Machen's vision of an unhappy family locked forever in a brown study by Sickert: the lobotomised ennui of Lazarus as a pre-condition of Hackney residence. The little death of London for those who are not free to roam.

In Kingsbury Road, Toate quickened his stride, going with the flow, accepting that he himself was being ridden now by old bricks, curtains of ivy, and penitential walls safeguarding the Jewish burial ground in which Amy Levy, the poet whose words still teased and echoed, was buried. "He comes," she wrote, "I hear him up the street." Those phrases again, but much closer to ground that was Levy's for eternity. And with more weight and consequence. "Bird of ill omen, flapping wide / The pinion of a printed sheet." Attempts to gain access here, the promise dangled before Lee, had been rebuffed. The site was insecure, stonecropped tombs in need of restoration. Pushed out and away from that stillness and silence, the wild nature of the forbidden enclosure, they drifted in a fugue, coming back to consciousness and the stated quest when they lost grip on the rope of memory and staggered into the maelstrom of Stoke Newington Road, old Ermine Street. Confirmed geographical points burnt like vivid stanzas in a poem still to be written. The orange halo from a single light bulb was not yet extinguished in the high window on the corner of Amhurst Road. Anna Mendelssohn's words circled and bit. "However close to the earth she goes, her imagining found no home."

Beaming at his return to familiar territory, Lee suggested a coffee in Toate's Dynevor Road attic, a nod to Conrad's mean retreat. But the heat of the hunt was too fierce: no digressions, no surrender. Toate, wincing from blisters on his blisters, gall to his kibe, raced north on the foretold path, dowsing the diminishing wake of previous failures. Was the side entrance to Abney Park, after they had detoured around the discontinued excavations of improvers, still Machen's "foretaste of infinity"? Was this the afternoon for locating the one and only vantage point from which the parallel experience of the enchanted Canon's Park would be made manifest? Look, stranger. And look again. It was never about place. It was about distance. It was about passing through a set of subtle radio beams, warning the Old Ones of this latest invasion.

The Machen disciples rejected all tried and tested neural pathways. There was no approach to the non-denominational and occulted shell of the church. No cap-in-hand bias towards the final resting place of Emily Gosse. No scrabble through thorn and bramble from a particular bench towards a particular memorial slab for the engraver Calvert, friend of Samuel Palmer. Find a tempting path and, when that forks, take another. The least appealing. And another, worse again. And another. Neither advancing nor retreating. Something never before attempted. "Green hollows bordered with thyme." Leaf mould squelching underfoot. The knotted fingers of overarching branches high above. The bore of a long green tunnel and a disk of burning light beyond. Stone angels lift their handless arms in warning. Lee remembered Powys: "He felt as if there were arising from that place of mortality a sweet, faint, relaxing breath, full of the deliciousness of luxurious dissolution." And in that self-conscious literary dissolution, he lost his moment and the ground beneath his feet. He was returned, deflated but unscathed, to his home, his duties and his desk. The Machen expedition was in overload. It never happened beyond the pages of the books on his shelf of prized first editions. The whole conceit of Canon's Park, Lee grasped, was that it should never be found. Or even lusted after.

Toate's swollen foot brushed against something feral moving swiftly through the undergrowth. His socks were sodden. They gave him no comfort. They were wet and *white*, sticky and sour. Milk? The escaping cat or rat or mole had tipped over a beer glass filled with sour milk. Several of the drowned flies floating there, spinning as the world spun, without hope, shuddered and shook themselves. They beat their wings with a sound like a miniature chainsaw. They flew into the air and fell and limped away. The podcaster watched their dripping trail. And then the pulse of his own life stalled.

"To infinity," he said. The hidden alphabet of flies and the networks of roots and intelligent mycelia were revealed in a blinding flash. And then withdrawn. Benches and broken angels were translated and transformed. *He had been right all along*: the vision in the private gardens of Gray's Inn was a perceptual trick, born of thwarted hopes and physical pain, the terror of existence. That beginning was also the end. It is one thing to see, or to imagine, or to write about the seeing, and it is another, entirely, to experience the great thing. *To be there in the seeing. And only there.* Toate was present in Canon's Park, a paradise garden with no walls and no gates. And beyond this garden, as he discovered, there was nothing at all: charring black smoke, darkness inside a greater darkness. A nauseous buzzing like fetal bones grinding in a soft skull, grinding and parting. Like bloody sawdust running from his ears. He had the park. He paid the price. There was no outside to this borderless inside. His tongue darted after salt. His arms were wings. His eyes bulged from his head. From his hiding place, he watched the white-skinned human stretch out on the bed. He could wait. He must wait. Veins pulsed in the sleeper's wrists. Come, brothers. Come, sisters. Come all. We will feast tonight.

LONDON SPIRIT

"No Chinaman must figure in the story."

– Ronald Knox,
Rules of Fair Play (for Detective Stories)

I n the bellying curve of that high window, like the captain's cabin of a timbered ghost ship, the short man stood, legs apart, polishing the clawing pangs of an empty stomach. *This was the winter of his seasonal discontent, but it was only a season. A brief initiation. And he would come through. There was a low green hum, not of remembered fields, of localised nuisance. Ancestral forces still to be tapped and exploited. Explained. Voices bigger and louder than the creatures producing them. Voices breaking language, their private language, into a mantic drone. The language of the cave. The clammy chill of unquarried stone. Of fossils that do not know they are fossils. The terminal beach where he found the horse's white skull. And carried it away.*

And now, so much worse, the silence. The straining after silence. Thunder of blood coursing in the canals of the ear. And the teasing interval before the hum begins again, above him, behind the heavy curtain, across the floor. Instructions he cannot interpret or endure.

Machen stood at his solitary window in London and stared at the pavement, at a single, leaf-printed York stone flag. 23 Clarendon Road, Notting Hill. A neutral rectangle of pearly grey, cut and smoothed. And laid with such precision, pressed down, so that the lip would not catch the step of a passing gentleman. After hours of paper and ink, clerical labours, this interval of standing. Of motionless meditation. Concentrating on one spot until it is ready to tilt. Until the old ones, the black riders, come. The splashed mud and the dung. Until the humming in the cabin becomes a prompt and he is released once more to chase the last rays of the setting sun. Machen makes a reflex sign of protection, third eye to navel to breast.

"Possessor of a cell no monk would envy, a small room measuring some ten feet by six." Other penitents and madmen raved behind other doors. There was a ladder to the roof and the stars. A Greek, so he reported, mated furiously with a chorus girl, until they shouted murder. A curse. On the house. The blood. On our broken polis. "A phase of misery and semi-starvation." Washed up on an island in London.

Machen endured whatever was necessary for vision. Strikes out: Turnham Green, Gunnersbury, and Kensal Green. "A place of early horror for the young man." Maida Vale, Paddington, Portobello Road: "they all led to Golgotha". Willesden, Harlesden, Wormwood Scrubs, and Hendon: an overwhelming but never declared mystery. Hills or mounds or shining pyramids more soul-shredding than anywhere in the Welsh Marches. "Bleached sepulchres, row on serried row."

It was the hour of the spirit lamp and the black kettle. That single flagstone, frosted in moonlight, held him. He was othered. Green tea and a promised pipe. The diurnal procession was done. The figure in the story never came. On the shelf, among so many dead books, a white horse's skull held down a loose sheaf of papers. So many first drafts. So many stalled beginnings. Machen knotted his fists. The white scar across the palm of his hand, a hidden stigma, throbbed. He never learnt from life. These were markings from another place, a pan removed from hot coals. He found the skull wedged tight *among limestone pavements, the jagged lunar landscape of the west. Forced, loosened. He carried the trophy to London. It was infested. It buzzed and sang. An incestuous tenement. Flies, too canny to be trapped by sugar or syrup, were hidden in the cavity of the absent eye. Finding an ancient recipe somewhere in an odd volume of Albertus Magnus, Machen boiled his pan of water until the windows dripped. Reaching through the steam, he dropped a flattened hedgehog, brought back from one of his nocturnal tramps, into bubbling water. The flies would be repelled. He must have muttered the wrong incantation. The creatures multiplied. Taking up permanent residence, they protested. They drained him, day and night. The white skull was their chosen instrument of torture.*

Possibly there are things in heaven and earth more dispiriting than hanging on, at the end of a long dark afternoon in November, in a book cellar under a concrete flyover, contemplating a drive across London, Notting Hill to Hackney, but I haven't experienced them. The presence of shelved books, ordered and arranged for sale in an ill-lit biblio-brothel, sucks out the will to continue. Companion volumes, old friends heaped in a personal library or writing room, kindle memories. They are active. They collaborate, intervene, and intrude on any literary endeavour. They require servicing. They throb and whisper. They are a kind of indulged celibate harem.

Books die in the horror of public neglect. They can be rescued. *They must be rescued.* Recharged. Slid into the place that is already waiting for them. They will revise texts that have not yet been written. Our task is unaltered. As Yeats declaimed in *A Vision*: "The living can assist the imaginations of the dead."

I was in theoretical business—another punt, another disaster—with the mysterious, ever moving, ever vanishing and reappearing personality known as Driffield. And, more to the purpose, with a funded newcomer to the trade, creeping towards respectability and a viable shop near Gloucester Road underground station: Mr. Nick Dennys. Grubbers in the subterranean depths had to serve their time waiting on ghosts, like courtiers on the battlements of Elsinore.

Nobody came. Turn and turn about, we put in a shift, wondering when the promised future would arrive. Volumes bought in good faith on my travels, predatory trawls through Britain, raids on Holland, Belgium, France, and the Channel Islands, were fated to dress an exhibition of fallible taste. In the terminal fugue of halogen solitude on a dying Saturday, faint tremors of action from the streets above reached us. There were distinct shivers as trains rumbled and traffic surged towards the promoted illusion of motorway freedom. I didn't need to look, I had already committed to memory the top shelf of "better" items that had failed when catalogued and were now available at knockdown prices to collectors and runners too busy to trouble themselves with some unadvertised hole in the ground. I was responsible for a group of first editions and presentation copies by authors associated with the area.

Folly! Delusion! I should have recalled the story Driffield told, while conning a free cup of coffee and a cheese roll, by feinting to pay with a fifty-pound note peeled from the top of a thick roll of fivers held in place with a red rubber band. Back in his anarchist youth, before the current pseudonym and the prison tonsure, he had been part of a commune running a free Notting Hill bookshop. He spent much of the week scavenging charity shops and junk pits, on the bicycle with the bulging panniers, gleaning choice stock with which to educate and delight local browsers. He would lift the consciousness of the unenlightened. But they spurned the deal. Nothing at all was too much to pay.

Even when he barked them inside, they fled. The offered exchange was patronising. Nothing comes of nothing. If you valued these dogs at zero, why should they bother? Why should they drag away your rejects?

The solid phantom on the stairs manifested like a shock cut in a moody British thriller. With no footfall, he was suddenly *there*. Perhaps he had always been there and it took a state of existential despair, psychosomatic resignation, to see him. This person was trapped between assignations, coming from a covert meeting, expunged from the official biography, towards an adulterous table booked in a screened corner of a favoured Covent Garden restaurant. Any degree of visibility hurt the man. It was his boast to be always approaching a frontier from the wrong side, documentation covered by Jesuits, canvas rucksack loaded with malaria pills, condoms, and an India paper novel by Stevenson or Conrad.

Sliding down the narrow companionway towards what he perceived as an entirely accidental destination, my visitor was a frozen frame of surveillance footage to be instantly deleted. Shabby white raincoat, collar turned up, hands in pockets. Face tilted to the shadows, camera misdirected to the polished shoes. This pass at anonymity only confirmed my potential customer's identity as a spook or former spook: if such a role is possible. I knew from experience that the man on the stairs was a bookshop professional. Nothing hurried, arrive three minutes before closing time. Catch the trader off-guard while he is preoccupied packing the books into boxes. The swiftest of scans to evaluate the status of the merchandise. Anything "roast beef", as Driffield used to say, anything too obviously conforming to book-fair tedium, anything superficially pretty, any leatherbound odd volumes, and he'd walk away. The wrong kind of antiquarian survivors shouldn't make it from the battlefield. There was enough here to hold the spectral bounty-hunter in his white surgical scrubs: modest fodder worth a second glance and a lick of the forefinger. But he must not succumb to a single giveaway twitch of excitement. Fancied items pushed back, reversed, spine hidden, like a dead letter drop in a Viennese cemetery. Graham Greene knew just how to play it.

We were the only living and breathing entities in the building. It was a classic Mexican standoff. Memories of *Lawless Roads*. Finding traces of primitive murals in a ruined chapel. Greene, steady hands in raincoat pocket, made a swift pass. He established that his nephew, Nick Dennys, his sister's boy, the one in whom he took an interest, was not on duty. He scanned the shelves that belonged to Nick, indulgently, without investigating a single volume. Then he slowed, intrigued but unconvinced by an item or two among my prized stock. *He would have to touch them.* It would be a near religious intervention. I saw the future catalogue entry: "Faint imprint of Graham Greene's thumb on front free endpaper". A sample of the DNA of the great man would be available: at a cheeky price. And if he was prepared to give me a cheque, with a tight but authentic signature, I'd offer him an immediate and generous discount.

Greene was far too canny for that. I stood off, pretending to take an interest in punk memorabilia on another stall, but tracking every move. And still I missed it. With a slight lisp of acknowledgement, the collectable author gathered up his condescending bundle. He had ignored a copy of his own first novel, *The Man Within*, published in 1929, and possessing a somewhat tired dust-wrapper; along with ill-advised restoration work spotted at once by his discerning eye. The famed entertainer stuck with the Victorian and pre-war novels of detection and lowlife. Items he pursued in competitive alliance with his brother Hugh.

Arthur Morrison's *Chronicles of Martin Hewitt* and *Tales of Mean Streets* (with loosely inserted ALS from the author, penned in Chalfont St. Peter): a good spot. Morrison letters are scarce and valued (but not here). G. K. Chesterton: *The Man Who Was Thursday*, an early reissue in spectacular jacket. Sax Rohmer: *The Dream-Detective*. First edition in jacket. I was sorry to part with that one, but I found it under the Westway flyover, and felt obliged to trade it back into the same area. *"When did Moris Klaw first appear in London? It is a question which I am asked sometimes and to which I reply: To the best of my knowledge, shortly before the commencement of the strange happenings at the Menzies Museum."*

There was no lamplighter exchange of paper or conversation. The chosen books were set aside, not for future collection (thankfully), nor for packaging and post: no address would be offered. Greene knew the market value of his faintest scribble. Sometimes he doctored ordinary books with the brief annotations that would make them worth cataloguing by his nephew. I was instructed to hold the items until I saw Nick again. He would make payment on his uncle's behalf. The old spy had reached the point in his career when he didn't have to put a signature to the letters he dictated.

It was a curious episode, our only meeting, and it stayed with me, a memory marker from another life. But it was no more curious, I suppose, than the threads of happenstance that brought Aileen, Kim Philby's estranged first wife, and Elisabeth, Greene's much loved youngest sister, to Crowborough, a sleepy Sussex town. Where their neighbours included the Catholic convert's wife and children, the ones he occasionally found time to visit, when he returned from distant lands. Or France. Elisabeth inducted Graham into MI6. The Secret State funded

feverish ventures in extreme African tourism. For a few
months in St. Albans, the author worked alongside Philby.
They continued to exchange correspondence after the
infamous flight to Russia. And Crowborough, as Greene
was well aware, was the dormitory where Sir Arthur Conan
Doyle lived out his final act, in a grand property thought
to be haunted.

All this is literary gossip now, steam on the saloon bar
mirror. After Elisabeth Dennys, a striking woman with
"blue, exophthalmic eyes", suffered a stroke at the wheel
of her car, Graham's own health began to deteriorate.
He arranged for the sale of his library and letters, to help
support Elisabeth and her family. He died in 1991.

That is, two years *before* I saw him hesitating on the
dark stairs, *before* he decided to complete his descent
towards the waiting shelves of books. And two years before
our brief exchange. And before the arrival of the digital
colonisation of the dirty old trade. Greene always said, and
it was a sustainable fantasy, that if he had not become a
professional writer, he would have dedicated himself to
antiquarian bookselling. The activities are inseparable.
There is a chiasma between writing, publishing, and
hawking. After my encounter with the dead man, I drifted
away from dealing and started producing fodder to clog
the shelves of other traders, items designed to disappear
with good grace.

Thinking back on this unreliable episode from a period
more remote than the Pleistocene, I began to wonder
about the interconnections between books with which we
have forged an intimate relationship and specifics of place.
Texts are conjured from dreams lodged deep in the terrain,
in landscapes imagined or associated with wherever we
happen to find ourselves at the point of sleep. The book

cellar was a ritual site, a cave shuddering beneath the elevated Westway and the railway. The hideaway trembled when east-west flow was spliced by the north-south transit of Portobello Road. Bored into a state of cortical shutdown at the end of a slack day's trading, I was ready to accept any infiltrating fetch. Hallucinations had escaped, like a mantle of sour gas, more smelled than observed, from the order of books on my Portobello shelf. If the spectre of Greene had been projected from *The Man Within*, could I expect—*if I returned to the location of the original visitation*—sightings of G. K. Chesterton, the Wyndham Lewis of *Rotting Hill*, and, most desired of all, the J. G. Ballard of *Concrete Island*?

When I folded up my shelves and decamped, back east, shortly after the summoning of Greene, I withdrew from sale a pristine copy of *Concrete Island*. A few years later when, along with our respective partners, I used to meet Ballard for a midweek meal in a restaurant of his choice, around Shepherds Bush, I braved his genial displeasure by asking him to sign it. He didn't have a pen, so I gave him mine. The spindly presentation inscription is made in the same pale red that I use to correct and annotate drafts of work in slow progress. It's that magic of touch again: the sentiment of a specific occasion preserved and made into an unholy relic. A pirate contract signed in blood.

The Ballard novel from 1974, middle volume of a dystopian trilogy, when I read it again in 2022, vividly demonstrated the author's gift for operating outside the constrictions of the space-time continuum. Narrative is pared right down, elegant in its essential minimalism. Language becomes a set of variable propositions. A speeding car—no camera fines then—comes off the Westway, dumping a heavyweight architect, in the throes of psychotic breakdown, on a prison island surrounded by unsecured embankments and a perimeter fence. The use of technical language—*caisson, culvert, pinion, glycol, chromium window trim*—cohabits, affectionately, with the poetics of bodily damage and psychological disintegration. The lush ecology of the island, sturdy grasses and ruins of previous civilisations, cinemas and air-raid shelters, is closer to *The Tempest* than to the acknowledged source in *Robinson Crusoe*. Maitland, the abdicated architect, finds his Caliban, along with a strung-out Miranda, who is father-fixated and moonlighting as a motorway prostitute.

If you choose to read it in that way, *Concrete Island* predicts everything in 176 pages. It honours a past that might or might not have happened. And is still happening. The precise location of the crash cannot be identified, it exists somewhere in Ballard's visionary cartography. But you are free to say that, in our imaginatively undernourished world, this drama plays out on a tease of liminal ground between the Westway, the M41 spur to Shepherds Bush, and the A40 Wood Lane, running south alongside the former BBC Television Centre. The dark kingdom of Jimmy Savile. A short drive, and a direct line, from the flat in Goldhawk Road, where Ballard routinely visited his friend, Claire Walsh; the scholarly woman who took care of his internet communications, and who accompanied him, at weekends, on his gallery visits and drives out to inspect the latest downriver interventions, the empty domes and retail parks.

You can nominate parts of *Concrete Island* that pretend to incubate horrors of recent times: ill-served tower blocks doomed by political incompetence and corruption, black smoke on the skyline, viral invasions. "Perhaps the source of a virulent plague had been identified somewhere in central London. During the night, as he lay asleep in the burnt-out car, an immense silent exodus had left him alone in the deserted city." Ballard's obsessive tropes move both ways in time, identifying malfate from scrambled reports on radio and in newsprint, but also channelling and finessing historic crimes. The reference to a police sergeant at Notting Hill urinating on the brain-skewed vagrant who shares the traffic island is a direct invocation of an attack launched on the writer Jack Trevor Story in that notorious nick. "You don't forget that kind of thing."

The concrete ramp, or launch pad into Ballard's perverse psychopathology, would have to be walked and investigated. The Westway had been identified early, and used whenever possible for his regular commutes between W12 and Shepperton. He called the theme park motorway, more aspiration than reality, "a poignant reminder of what might have been". It afforded fictional architects a passing view of "some of the most dismal housing in London". Back at the start there were few surveillance cameras. "You can make your own arrangements with the speed limits," Ballard wrote. "Like Ankor Wat, the Westway is a stone dream that will never awake."

The steel and tarmac exoskeleton, three-miles long, a fragment from a discontinued future, is the neural slipway between fiction and reality. The written truth of the old masters, however wild and speculative, has more heft than the self-serving prevarications of politicians and planners. Take for example the case of author and visual essayist Chris Petit. One year before Greene died, Petit made a short film with Ballard for *The Moving Motion Picture Show*. When Chris came to publish his first novel, *Robinson*, he opened with an epigraph from Ballard. "Deep assignments run through all our lives; there are no coincidences." Petit's narrator, after a heavy session in Soho, is handed the keys to a Jaguar. He is ordered to drive towards the Westway. Lacking personal volition, drifting through a nightworld, as film hack and under-the-pavement bookseller, this man has no choice but to become absorbed in the slipstream of *Concrete Island.* He climbs aboard the very car that Maitland was driving: foot down to cemetery or asylum.

"I was well over the limit and drunk enough not to care." Petit's *Robinson* must be returned to source, to Defoe. He will make a Ballardian road movie rather than a Situationist walk to Stoke Newington, as devised by Patrick Keiller for his film, *London.* "The car seemed to drive itself . . . We cruised past Warren Street, jumped red lights on the Euston Road and hit eighty on the Westway with Robinson hooting with laughter and shouting 'Faster, faster!' as the speedometer crept towards a hundred."

Asked about "coincidences", Petit said that all he wanted to do was get a car and camera out on the Westway. He felt the compulsion to take a good hard look at Ballard's locations. As if the fact of Ballard deciding to write about this stretch made it his own urban parkland in perpetuity. Returning there, back across town from Hackney, like one of my earlier bookselling commutes, would be the best chance of meeting and talking again to the late and fondly remembered Shepperton author. One of the terse, fast-moving chapters in *Concrete Island* was called "The Perimeter Fence". Which was also the title Petit gave to his epic, multi-part, multi-media attempt, commissioned or self-funded, to re-map and reclaim aspects of British culture.

I launched my literary ghost hunt at Royal Oak, close enough to the source of the Westway. The concrete viaduct carried a perpetual stream of policed and frustrated traffic, high above the streets of lost or regenerated villages. I had planned to experience the recently promoted Elizabeth Line, from Whitechapel to Paddington, but those trains are fundamentalist: they don't run on Sundays.

I let the other passengers decant, while I dug out my maps and camera, and took my bearings. On the far side of the tracks there was a reef of peeling Paddington flats, straight out of Lucian Freud and the 1950s. Looking north, I caught my first glimpse of the putative urban motorway. And the walls and security barriers that divided me from it. Beyond the first banks of graffiti-sprayed brickwork, the hispid obstacles, buddleia and thorn offered a scrap of wasteground sympathetic to the colouring of Ballard's seductive fable.

The only human left on the platform was a man of indeterminate status; railway official or non-combatant traveller too late for his appointment with a through-express suicide. Pacing to the edge and back, he oozed clerical melancholy, buttressed by Victorian reserve and decorum. With his thinning scalp and cultivated moustaches, he suggested Thomas Hardy. But what did Hardy have to do with Westbourne Green? I was not yet sufficiently tuned to the vibrations of the tracks. Hardy flowed back along the steel ladder of the railway to King's Cross and the clearance of graves at Old St. Pancras churchyard. Collateral damage for the confident expansion of the burgeoning transport system.

After I had walked for a spell under the motorway, trying to gauge the measure of Maitland's fear, the hysterical delusions of *Concrete Island*, when he contemplates storming blind through an underpass tunnel, I returned to the shady avenue, the mature trees, of Westbourne Park Villas. There was the bright blue plaque set like a porthole into the elegance of a white wall: Thomas HARDY 1840-1928 Poet & Author Lived here 1863-1874. Subsisting as an architectural journeyman, Hardy kept morbid anomie in check by reading John Stuart Mill's *On Liberty*.

There is room to breathe here, a complacency of means and managed resources running in parallel, but screened from, the vulgarity of railway and elevated road. Contrasting streams of time are never tempted to overlap or cohabit. The 1960s admix of Notting Hill freeloaders, libertarians with small private incomes, SF experimentalists, and many strands of immigrant, celebrated in the high days of Moorcock and Ballard and *New Worlds*, was almost out of reach. Almost, but not quite. I was not a camera, but I made a documentary note of *People on Sunday*: street brunches, community events in former churches, preoccupied single gentlemen carrying dogs. A public artwork, a hollow figure, like an unstuffed Wicker Woman holding an open book, was a votive sacrifice to a zone of privileged history. I knew this place only from ill-advised visits to collapsing publishers, meetings with old hippies rebranded as financial advisers, from screenings, dinners, Tarot readings, but I didn't know it at all. I had not paid close attention to the overnight changes in the gardens, the new people at new forms of leisure, the latest generation of retro-curating street peddlers. I knew Notting Hill like I knew Ostend, Cologne, Palermo, Cork: an interested tourist on a week's commissioned research (with honorarium). I sat on an ivy-smothered lip of stone among the civic plantings. The church building, detached from doctrine and function, was a site of pilgrimage. Mad theories, justifications for one day's excursion, bubbled and seethed. The dead return as estate agents. Ghosts have their dealers, their agents demanding fifteen percent of the action. Post-code gangs excavate basement swimming pools.

Noticing, as I approached the junction with Portobello Road, a sign for Powis Gardens, I decided to make a short detour, paying my respects to the Roeg/Cammell film,

Performance, by identifying the "right" house in Powis Square: number 25, not 80, as the film deploys. If there could be anywhere *physical* for the sub-cultural signifiers of a Jerry Cornelius multiverse to play out their potent myths, this was it. Mick Jagger, Anita Pallenberg, James Fox. Borges and Burroughs. Christine Keeler, Mandy Rice-Davies. Profumo and Peter Rachman, along with his celebrity enforcer, Michael X: they are all present, all dissolving into a series of pastiched Francis Bacon paintings of homo-erotic violence and submission. Ballard's crashes and atrocity exhibitions are leaking into every valid mews and dimension.

There had been a great collision, at which I had been a silent witness, when Ballard and Nicolas Roeg coincided in a Chinese restaurant, where they both thought they could rely on a predictable menu and guaranteed invisibility. The old colonialists, in equal measure courteous and lethal, socially expansive when it suited them, private when it didn't, were grooved to their routines. Favoured eating places operated like the gentlemen's clubs around which they steered a wide arc. Both of them looked and sounded establishment, established in counter-intuitive subversion. In high risk and originality. They knew one another, of course, and Roeg had been a strong contender when *Crash* was floated as the production that could never be brought to the screen. But on this particular evening, when Roeg was dining early with a young woman, the two men postponed mutual acknowledgement, the formal stand-up exchange, as long as possible. Coming together for a few awkward pleasantries was really too much for my picture of the vanished world: those twinned artists were aspects of the same thing. They enjoyed the same cultic status. Edgar Allan Poe's William Wilson meets his persistent and annoying double: which one blinks first?

Paused, before crossing to the steps of the *Performance* house, where some rock recluse and a coven of drugged lovers was still in occupation, I snapped a photograph of a horse's head wedged in the railings of Powis Square. From nowhere—or Thomas De Quincey?—a Chinaman appeared. "Take it, please. It is yours, yes. Take it away."

The elongated skull was wrapped in dog fur. Thick lips stretched over a sneering grin and a soft wet tongue. The horse's skull was fixed on a stick. It could have been chucked out at carnival time or left behind after a kiddies' party in the square. The Chinese gentleman, the one who assumed responsibility for the trophy, rushed away. I accepted the role assigned to me, but held the stick in such a way as to make it seem as if the hobby horse was tracking me like a stray pet. I understood the darker implications of this contract. My mother's family, back in Wales, looked after the Mari Lwyd: a white horse's skull buried on a moonless night. Then excavated and dressed with red ribbons for New Year's Eve. The shamanic totem, representing the spirits of the returning dead, was processed around the houses of the village, by drunks and revellers. They chorused a poetic challenge to those inside. When the challenge was not returned, rude intruders broke into the warm shelter, to be given drink and Teisen Lap at the fireside.

"Mari Lwyd, Horse of Frost, Star-horse, and White Horse of the Sea, is carried to us," the poet Vernon Watkins wrote. "The Dead return . . . They strain against the door . . . The Living, who have cast them out, from their own fear, from their own fear of themselves, into the outer loneliness of death, rejected them, and cast them out for ever . . . Drunken claims and holy deceptions."

Watkins said that what he wanted was to bring together those that had been separated. Where there was no separation. Where every night's candlelit labours, family abed, brought the voices of the drowned, the villagers lost beneath the sea, to his bungalow door.

Across the road from the Electric Cinema, where Ballard came to doze quietly through a screening of a road trip circumnavigating the M25 motorway, a young woman from an ethical café presented me with a thimble of iced coffee made from oats and grains, but without coffee or ice. I tracked Ballard but he wasn't there. I needed to return to the book cellar under the flyover. There was some encouragement in the stylish calligraphy of a pub that boasted of being "Home of London Dry Gin and Proud Purveyors of London Spirit".

The London Spirit of former times had decamped. The book bunker where I laboured no longer felt like a forcible exile on Hadrian's Wall, the site was hipped with vans and traders. The Westway pressed hard on the roof of the building in which I had guarded a communal stall. The present motorway caves were the caissons Ballard loved to describe. Some of the Sunday hawkers even looked like escapees from *Concrete Island*. Where once I had scooped from the floor a copy of David Gascoyne's *A Short Survey of Surrealism* (and kept it), along with a first edition of John Lennon's *In His Own Write*, signed by all the Beatles, their partners of the moment and Helen Shapiro (sold, far too soon), there was now a respectable and nicely set out arrangement of book tables with all the interest of a shelf of polished pebbles. No oddball intruders, no sleepers. Every item was internet evaluated. The big sleep of authors of uncompleted masterpieces must never be disturbed. They should not be called back to this place, on some dank winter evening, by a bored bookseller or a stalking phantom.

As drained of momentum as the market site in which intimations of earlier times were more persuasive than anything I thought I witnessed now, I let the steady drip of a leaking past become an amniotic flood. The elevated railway and the concrete Westway were roof beams over a tolerated amphitheatre of resurrected chaos. This was not and never had been my brand of chaos, but it was powerful. "Under the flyover" was an accepted anarchist rendezvous, a portal offered to accredited dealers. And weekend visitors with cash in hand. Under the rattle and screech of the trains, the susurration of traffic, there was another, wilder sound: a troop of pirate musicians, headbangers, stoned and stamping, rattling their rings and bangles, tossing hair. Hawkwind were tribalising the territory with urban chants. Mike Moorcock, kindred spirit, willing accomplice, was present, a link to Ballard. "We weren't looking for peaceful," the band spokesman said, "we were looking for horrid. We lock the doors and have the strobes pointed out at the crowd. We used to give them epileptic fits. We used to fuck people up good." And the people loved it. Grinning beatifically as they writhed in the dirt.

Beneath the elfin gardens of Tolkien colonists, beneath that minatory Westway lid, there was derangement and violence. Terraces torn down. "Destruction in Art" symposia attended by outpatients and anoraks with bulky recording machines. There was acrid smoke from burning towers of books fired by John Latham or Gustav Metzger. There were dead donkeys, dead people. The unregistered and unloved hid themselves in the rubble where travellers and thieves laid out their wares on filthy blankets. And where dandies from the wrong century stalked and dealt. Jerry Cornelius, Moorcock's pop-art assassin, drank port and lemon with old ladies and listened to their tales. If Hawkwind could be called the "People's Band", they didn't simply dress a set: they emerged from it. Like a summons. Dues paid, they belonged. And the people, not loveable, but always generous in disaffection, cast no votes in their favour.

Moorcock with his Odessa cap and revolutionary Russian beard began as a shed drummer in a South London suburb, before swapping a collection of lead soldiers for a proper guitar. He skiffled in Soho, but his abiding passion was for Delta blues. In Paris, between plagues and strikes, he recorded a final collaboration with a courteous but wasted Nicholas Lane: two of the great bookman prophets, channelled and channelling, trying to keep regular appointments in a recording studio. Moorcock would complete the project on his own. "In the case of sonic attack on your district," he wrote for Hawkwind, "follow these rules . . . Use your wheels, it is what they are for . . . Survival means every man for himself . . . There will be bleeding from orifices . . . You may be subject to fits of hysterical shouting . . . Your only protection is flight."

There were caves revealed by the construction of the Westway. Spaces for community projects and free gigs. Moorcock joined Hawkwind for a "motorway concert". He wrote the lyrics for "John Dee's Song". He registered the sinister clouding in the scrying glass. "In my skull's a multiplicity of spheres / An infinity of Albions." All rattling to get out. To join the party at the end of time.

The Ballard trilogy was being enacted within a smaller and smaller reach of ground. The couplings and perversities of *Crash* were above the heads of the market mob and, simultaneously, trolling down slip roads to a game reserve of wrecked cars and survivalists in cellars. Out on the embankment rim a burning and blackened tower was presently occupied by ordinary accidental humans, in place of the cannibal architects and warring hierarchies, the psychotic technocrats of Ballard's downriver fiction.

Having come so far, travelling back rather than forward, by tapping familiar ghosts, remembering in the solitude of a walk through the Sunday market stories told over and again, I branched away from Westbourne Park and Ladbroke Grove to Clarendon Road—with the notion of acknowledging the perch once occupied by the young but never youthful Arthur Machen.

A step too far? Spheres within spheres. Contemporary Clarendon Road is muffled in the silence of money. I stooped to photograph the only rectangular flagstone clear of fallen leaves. There was a craftsman publisher I knew, a man who gathered up grasses, acorns and twigs to be pressed and macerated into pulp, from which he would manufacture the paper for special editions. He wasn't above throwing in the odd crisp packet, for added colour. This section of pavement was another kind of book. More on the Anselm Kiefer scale: too heavy to lift and bereft of words. Gravid with its own pseudo-historic dignity.

There was absence in Machen's window. On my return home, I had to spend hours with a magnifying glass trying to read this mysterious photographic capture. To get beyond the illusion when the sudden flash of the camera offended the calm of the morning. And that more troubling illusion: a dark figure at the window staring down at me. I lost myself in reflections of an enchanted garden with much bluer skies than anything in the neighbourhood. Bare bricks instead of the freshly painted plaster. And a fluted column that did not quite connect with a nameless marble plaque.

Nobody looked out. Nobody had ever occupied this room. The proportions made no sense, fittings floated free. When I pulled back for a wider shot, the window became a set of panels in slate. It was a good house from which to break away. The door would be locked against any return. A sticker had been wrapped around the black pole of a pedestrian crossing with a little green man: THE EARTH IS FLAT. I had reached my limits. Another step and I would find myself signing on for an excursion advertised in Holland Park with its bookshops, delicatessens and artisan bakers: KARL MARX WALKING TOUR.

Ballard walked here in memory and therefore in fact. He skulked across the road from his favoured parking spot, to a meeting room reserved for interviews in the Hilton Hotel. Pressured too long by a photographer, on a traffic island in a thunderstorm, he called the session to an abrupt conclusion and marched off—bumping into Machen, as the late Victorian spectre flinched from intimations of the Westfield shopping centre, the furies in their unspeakable metal chariots, the sinister corridors and studios of the BBC enclave with their licensed predators and unquiet histories.

The child's horse that I still clutched was becoming a problem. It was impatient to get me back to Portobello Road. I rammed the fur-covered skull into the hedge around a neighbourhood patch of shade, where it caught the attention of a local character with comedy aspirations. He pounced on the prop. He laughed. Dirty nails scratched sparks from greying stubble. He did the Eric Morecambe schtick with his horn-rimmed spectacles. But, most significantly, he talked to the beast, squeezing the long snout against his ear. Evidently, the oracular creature spoke back. Expecting an Irish lilt, I was surprised by the Old Etonian drawl of the equine confidence trickster. And shocked by a trickle of blood running from his nose.

"Your nag is the bollocks. Is he standing in the leadership election?" The man in the checked shirt was getting into his act. "I thought you were carrying a dead cat with a pole up its arse," he said. "You look like a person in unwelcome receipt of hypnagogic jactitation."

North of Chesterton Road, the urban buzz died down. I lost the Ballardian afterburn of the Westway and *Concrete Island*. The mood was elegiac. "Paradise By Way of Kensal Green", said the pub sign, nodding to that premature and jovial Brexiteer, Gilbert Chesterton. "For there is good news yet to hear and fine things to be seen, / Before we go to Paradise by way of Kensal Green."

Coming off Harrow Road, I found a bench in the cemetery. What a very strange sculptural relief that had been on the panel above the door of the pub. The naked legs and buttocks of a woman being swallowed into the gaping maw of a vegetative gorgon. A foliate head. Here was an eccentric vision of a green paradise conjured from somewhere between a gargoyle on a twelfth-century Romanesque church and a lascivious doodle by G. F. Watts. In Kensal Green, we were back among flights of grounded angels with decorative but inadequate wings. Someone had left a black beret, smelling of Gauloises Caporal cigarettes and ten-year-old Armagnac, on the bench beside me.

I recalled the memorial service here, with jazz, poetry and fond reminiscence, for the double-identity writer, Robin Cook/Derek Raymond. The ceremony and the wake that followed at the French House on Dean Street marked the end of an era. Robin was a person of consummate charm, a teller of tales, some of them his own.

Under the jaw of the horse was a leather pouch. Perhaps a hiding place for the key to all these mysteries? A secular phylactery? I felt inside and my groping fingers discovered a cold black metallic object: a battery cylinder with a switch. Before I risked activation, I put the beret on the horse's head, where it felt quite at home. I pressed the skull in the obvious places, hoping for speech. I whispered the names of Greene and Chesterton and Ballard with no result. Then, in frustration, I pulled out the still damp tongue and the head spoke in a voice I recognised. A speech I had heard Robin Cook deliver at the City Airport in Silvertown, on his return from Paris.

"The dead, their faces remain in my mind much longer than the faces of living people . . . They say the dead don't come back. Sometimes I'm glad when they do and sometimes I wish they didn't. But they come anyway . . . You can't keep the dead out . . . They rest on your shoulder, whatever you're doing, they weigh *nothing*. Not a feather of weight. But they have no new word to say. It's always the same thing. 'Join us.' The river is open. I speak to them and they speak to me."

Join us. I was travelling the wrong way. Nobody was coming back to this place. After three miles of the Westway, up there on the stilted heights, or tramping in the shadows with the derelicts, concrete fails and the runway lifts into the clouds, into the far west. Radio off. Eyes shut. Skin flushed with expectation. *Join us.*

You can tramp for as many hours as your legs will carry you, but you cannot break the leash. Every expedition carried Machen to the same bench in Kensal Green Cemetery: Golgotha! His arm, under the sweated linen, the layers of wool, itched. An angry red line traced the vein. Blood taken by the messenger fly, to be passed on to some other unsuspecting host. Dreaming our days. Living our nights. On the treadmill of necessity. A stone garden, guarded by calcified angels, across the canal from Gas Works and hospital. Machen nibbled a few crumbs of gingerbread. The grandiose sepulchres and pyramids, the empty family mausoleums, did not shine. And the writer could not pass on to the underworld or the places beneath the hills. He shouted but they did not hear. That was what drew him back to the enclosure with its hollow architecture, its temples and anchored angels. The dawning certainty that he was now the spectre, restless, with many stories still to be told. The things he saw stayed here forever. Until, in their turn, they too became phantasmagoric. He did not recover, through walks or long nights of study, glimpses of previous beings. He was the previous, the dead and dying future. And those visitors would trespass in his imagination as he would trespass in theirs. And the cycle would continue. The flies were the emanations of this unfortunate pathology. The fever to which he was addicted.

NO
WAR

AT THE MOUNTAINS OF MADNESS

"Great things are done when Men & Mountains meet
This is not done by Jostling in the Streets."

– William Blake

Time-coded at two hours and forty minutes after he
died, I received a message on my duncephone from
the poet and painter whose work and personality
had affected all our lives. London Spirit was dispersed,
smoke from a bottle, and there was no resolution, this time,
in simply walking away. Walking blindly on and on until
inspiration bit afresh. And fingers twitched to grip a pen.
He wanted to talk and he would talk, in a different register,
and I would have to remain alert to catch the implications of
that gravel-gargling, whisky-lubricated, breathless voice, at
once intimate and impossibly far away. The stubby burner
phone is almost fashionable again, a paging device only to
be activated when I'm on the road and need to be security
tagged in case of anticipated emergencies at home, or that
inevitable moment when event overwhelms the exhausted
myth of an independent self kept apart from the flypaper
morass of the city. Our biology does not function outside
the skin of the world. I was no longer a doppelgänger in
pursuit of a host in pursuit of me.

The Freedom Pass does not become freedom, on my
laminated card, until the hour when sensible Hackney folk

have completed their exercise regimes and moved on, primed and wired, to faux industrial spaces where they will fire up waiting screens. How soon does the day's excursion become a quest and the quest a new chapter? Innocent of devices, I heard, somewhere in the prison of the skull, that pre-ordained and pillow-smothered voice reciting words from the Book of Revelation, words too portentous for innocent delivery: "I saw a new heaven and a new earth: for the first heaven and the first earth were passed away; and there was no more sea. And I John saw the holy city, new Jerusalem, coming down from God out of heaven, prepared as a bride adorned for her husband."

A recipe dusted down for the death of kings. An old country in a fouled sea, exhausted, shamed, giving up her parade of heritaged ghosts. Universally cancelled. Amen. And good riddance. Golden glimpses are only licensed when the abyss is yielding her grinning monsters. And the hills are on fire. The oceans enraged.

I was going down, deeper and deeper, in order to access this newly delayed and fabulously over-budget train: hence the voices. The madness in the head. What happened to all that soil? Landslides and fat bergs and river terrace deposits, sifted discriminations of gravel, silt, sand, and clay? What happened to the chattering plague bones, the tatters and rags and toys of rich and poor? Where did they take the collateral damage, the spoil of the city? How did they ameliorate psychic disturbance? Without the sad duvet of those resting layers, memory deposits, what anchored the jostling surface, the wind-making, sharpened towers of maximum visibility and zero substance? Surface noise was unbearable, agitated flocks of willing screen slaves, screeching lovers, debt dodgers, collisions in transit. Tangled leashes, horns, challenges, rubber on tarmac, metal on flesh.

Here were apocryphal gospels for an age without doctrine. I was descending without moving, hanging on. As to final judgement. Into the maw of the beast whose silvered throat opens like a shark, rivets for teeth. Everything is steel blue. Ribs of a customised theme park whale. A gigantic condom. Elective Jonah wanting to be spat out, at the end of the nightmare journey, into some desert place beyond the limits of our feeble imaginings. PLEASE STAND ON THE RIGHT. REMEMBER NOT ALL DISABILITIES ARE VISIBLE.

Glass doors open with a surgical hiss. Like gas under pressure, underwater. The train is so long that there are seats for all classes, apart from those who choose to walk, without appreciating that this is a new form of transit admitting no poverty spectres from former Whitechapel picaresque. Up above us, the standing skeleton is still in its vitrine, with fearsome beekeeper's hat and veil, secured for students in the medical museum. But the Elephant Man, insulted by inappropriate terminology, has departed. Another hospital more like a Hilton hotel has been laptop generated on top of the old heroic butchery sheds. Photographic albums of local record have been laid aside: "history" is an uncertain resource to be thoroughly laundered and sanitised before release. Joseph Merrick's vision clouds the glass and oversees the demolition and removal of the sacred Mound that once protected a rebel city from royalist canons and courtiers. It was excavated, carted and dragged away, shipped downriver to landfill dunes at Rainham, freeing us to re-imagine a new Jerusalem, adorned like a mail-order bride. There is a natural history of destruction better left untouched. And unwritten.

The carriage supplicant, announced in a generous swirl of impregnating odour creeping ahead of him like the lousy vest of John the Baptist, knows that he is in the wrong place at the wrong time. The previous new trains, post-Olympic, on the Overground loops, advised, in concerned and responsible tones, that any temptation to conspicuous coin-drop charity should be sidetracked into approved channels. On no account should desperate beggars, driven to this debasing (for all parties) humiliation, be trusted with a small personal pension to waste on the frivolities of survival. Such acts would only encourage an infestation of professional mendicants. As if the compulsion to work a pitch, to hold out a grubby hand, was an easy thing, a career of choice. Favoured hustlers, with their unearned dividend, might blow the lot on a regime of self-administered medication or firewater to get them through another day, a long cold London night. This thin young man's heart was not in it. He spoke like a voice box in a stuffed monkey, pulled with a short string. "You guys . . . " No gender discrimination. It is the women who used to reach out, with churchy reflex, in the days when there were still coins in the bag. "Spare a little change. Please."

I fumble in my knitted Peruvian pouch, but he's gone before I can feel for the heptagon of a small coin of choice. Before I can stroke the relief profile of the last monarch's crowned head. The beggar has evaporated. In the afterburn of his own furies. In the certain knowledge that all permissions are cancelled beyond Liverpool Street. The Elizabeth Line sadhu is a spectre of the true east, of poverty barracks and opium dens, of squats and ruins and the mulch of vanishing street markets. His astral twin lingers and is not dispersed before Farringdon Road, where I have to exit. This man should be sponsored as a reminder of reality. Bad sleep in wet cardboard and bin liners. In the verminous scratch of dead tobacco underwear. In a coatless Siberia heated by resentment and cheap palliatives. He does not register among the millions of digital prompts and flickers on those miniature screens, those marvels of addictive technology, where ghosts never fade. And are always many kilowatts brighter than life.

The hope of a few loose coins among the threads was buried by the weight and mass of the book I was carrying. It was my fetish, when out on the road, to transport, as a sort of penance, a volume that could be left in place of something novel and provocative, picked up from one of the free exchanges proliferating across over-civilised districts of the inner city, among railway terminals in freshly excavated development zones. Saint Augustine's *City of God* had been with me, barely broached, for a couple of years, since that delightful summer morning when it had been waiting for a willing student, on the buttock-darkened wood of a pew in a pilgrim church, a few yards from the roar of the indifferent motorway.

"Our present concern is with those demons whose special characteristics have been listed by Apuleius, situated between gods and men, belonging to the 'animal' species, with a rational mind, a soul subject to passions, a body made of air, a life-span of eternity . . . He attributes to men three contraries: a lowly abode, mortality, and misery."

Now that tag from the Sixties, a premature slogan before the age of slogans, has to be adjusted: "You are what you read." A non-specific insult to the thin mantle of protection that surrounded us, our bodies made of meat and dung, ran out ahead of the bookish traveller, of the train that was so long that it reached the next stop before leaving the last. Every mortgaged breath, at this late stage of life's torment, was borrowed from another and better writer's mouth. Every act was predictable but not preventable.

The self-ejected traveller, climbing smoothly without effort, beyond the need to tighten his hold on the germ culture of the moving balustrade, was elated to step outside, into the unedited morning. Into a part of London with so many prompts, so many misremembered adventures.

Farringdon Road was a portal: the library, the meat market, hospital and pilgrim church, the Fleet River accompanist. The point where a day's journey, a life's direction, has to be decided. Now, ambition channelled into the snap decision to step across some newly pedestrianised runway of risk, the traveller experiences a wave of the purest contentment. The echoes in his fuddled head were from another place, an earlier time when his nerves were sandpapered and raw and receptive. "The street is a void in the sequence of man." And so it was. The coffee-bearing beaker people, the swishing ponytails and the slouching hoods: they marched. Towards borrowed desks at which they could repudiate the sentiment of localism. "A void" became "avoid". The traveller passed under the welcoming Underground sign, converting horizontal drift to vertical purpose, as the buckled metal carpet swept him down towards a new system, a railway dedicated to dispersal, to retreat. "Those who walk heavily," the poet said, "carry their needs."

The new experience of the old line, less burdened with promotions, deserved its working boast: *Metropolitan*. The clients were few but respectful of the privilege of smooth progress, with brief blackout punctuation, like intertitles on a silent film: short tunnels engineered to emphasise the next episode of sunshine, the brighter parks and garden suburbs. Mothers with active infants thinned out, leaving the carriage to students of all ethnicities, all levels of engagement, in default transit to institutions that had replaced factories and warehouses where they might once have laboured. I sat, back to the view, ransacking my woven pouch, in quest of photocopies of earlier photocopies of wordless pages sick with unjustified images.

A woman whose family, traders of consequence, lost everything in Ethiopia, had brought something back, to carry her through a pinched childhood. She brought back stories: island-hopping around the Aegean, border-crossing, transit camp to forest, through the Balkans, through Hungary, Germany, Sweden, Finland, towards covert refugee status in world cities, in Paris, London, and New York. What she husbanded, close to the heart, were a couple of distressed prints attributed to the merchant and former poet, Arthur Rimbaud. The sulky boy with the mussed hair and fouled neckwear became a coffee trader. The early-modernist walker, the language pirate and rough-sleeping provocateur, anticipated another strand of an all-conquering world vision: the selfie! This woman, future exile, guarded the poet's self-portrait as a premature artisan barista. His words, blood in the throat, became advertising copy on sealed bags from cloud jungle farms; on packages so over-designed, every bean burnished like a golden coin, that the ethical producers could afford to plant a tree in respect of every purchased item. Rimbaud, in his asylum whites, glared like an assassin and pulled the trigger. Only revealing the place and the life that had trapped him in the wrong story. Revealing the cost of giving yourself so early to language. He had stripped poetry to the status of a technical report.

The young woman, lost daughter, homeless at home, taking the name of Alba Zutique, dedicated herself to reversing the Frenchman's trajectory and thereby sending time into a delirious vortex, in which she would be permitted to shuck off colonialism and exploitation, and to arrive, by way of poverty, hunger and monumental marches, at a crisis of vision. A crisis in which one city, one halogen night, would become all cities, unpeopled and definitively posthumous. And beyond the phrase making that also forged the true consciousness of high imperialism—"The official acropolis surpasses the most colossal conceptions of modern barbarity"—was a naked image. Was the anticipation of the culture of the blink. The smart screen ideogram. The machine dictating the message: Consume. Upgrade. Devour.

At Wembley Park, the traveller interpreted the halo of the national stadium, a teasing bow of calcified light, as a memorial to all the bricks and steel and rubble and noise that had been removed, to be transported and dumped by a convoy of lorries. An era of impure amateurs, make-and-mend Olympics, of newsreel cup finals, and exhibitions of Empire, was lost. The symbolism of the Twin Towers was decommissioned two years after the hijacked Islamist planes flew into the monoliths of the World Trade Center in New York City.

On his lap, and spread across the neighbouring seats of the empty carriage, prints of prints: Alba's testament to her travels. Beyond filthy window panels, more suited to a submarine than a train, a panorama of suburbs ambitious of becoming edgelands. Many have essayed their troubled pilgrimages, many have found inspiration. Alba, with her camera slung around her neck in place of a crucifix, made the pictures. Illuminations for a text yet to be written, never to be written. And already forgotten.

There were many sheets of legal contract, many finessed biographies and author photos, but no hard commission, no credits. You could work for three or four years, unsalaried, on a project you thought had been agreed, pimped by a smooth talker long since decamped to a once friendly hideaway re-imagined into democratic open plan offices in which all are equally unequal. All slaves. Corporations swallow corporations. Viruses cull percentage-harvesting agents. But, somehow, the content providers persist. The candle of ego flickers and it is not quite extinguished.

"A couple of thousand words," the email said. "To ballast the pictures. Looks better with a block of text at the back. Nobody is going to read it, but it adds tone. We'll do a nice job on her book, believe me, proper paper, proper design, Germany, plenty of white space. So: no dates, no titles! No bullshit footnotes. Fill a page but DO NOT on any account DESCRIBE what you THINK is there. This is NOT a fucking CATALOGUE. Payment, subject to approval and editorial revision, house style, on publication."

If there was an office, the person touting the job was never in it. Out of the country. Between book fairs. No matter how swiftly the traveller bashed out his reply to some urgent query, the message would always bounce back. Email address invalid. But the Zutique portfolio worried him. The images were unplaced, unjustified. They seethed with latent hostilities. There were domestic objects you might associate with certain hours of the day, with twilight or dawn. There was a pre-traumatic microclimate of elective malfunction. There were breaks in brooding thunderclouds, red streaks reflected in oil-smeared windows. Glycerine droplets, from the unblinking eyes of a plaster Madonna, wormed down a plump pink cheek. There was coherence without chronology. Alba was not a stalker, nor a stitcher of fraudulent elegies. Her city was about dissolving the pretensions of cities. Beyond *The City of God*, beyond human interference, the thing we call "nature" threw up its mountain ranges, on a scale impossible to quantify, on the borders of everywhere. Mountains promising volcanic eruption. Memories of steel-engravings promiscuously fingered in the odd volumes of childhood.

Alba had recorded earthworks, spiral-path mounds never laid out in accordance with the tenets of any known religion or belief system. You might as well purchase a spade and a facemask and set out to dig a tunnel into Lewis Carroll's

Wonderland. These mammary shapes, alarmingly lit, might be overgrown nuclear silos, colliery slag heaps, land art. They were not captures for a London guidebook or souvenirs from a blog by some Uxbridge psychogeographer.

To reach the heights, Alba excavated. She dug deep with unvarnished talons. Having recorded with magnifying lenses the creases in resistant globes of chewing gum and the emerald radiance in moss growing from the flaring nostrils of John Bunyan in Bunhill Fields, the photographer gave up her notion that forensic interrogation could provide answers to questions other forms of reportage would never satisfy. These were the prints I laid out as the Metropolitan Line train approached Harrow-on-the-Hill.

Alba concluded, it was now obvious, that she should abandon her attempt to catalogue everything that *resisted* photography. She would, like the man in the famous Calvino story, stop photographing the loved one or items touched by the hand of the loved one. The hand that touched her. She was forced to admit the impracticality of fixing the texture of a sleeper's face. From that point on, she lived from a suitcase stuffed with the residue of flights across Europe. She photographed and re-photographed, on a daily basis, the same exhausted set of prints. She quite liked the shape of the shivering leaf helmet of a particular tree in a Hackney street. She liked a scatter of Tarot cards blown across a wet pavement. But with each repetition, in the chain of precise locked-off captures, something was lost and something was gained. New blemishes were achieved. Old blemishes re-evaluated. Detail faded. The specific was soon elevated into the general. But, at the end of it all, no escaping the conclusion, she had identified her theme in an arrangement of mysterious mounds, dunes, or refuse pyramids. Like ripples of sound rescued from the silenced rubble of considerate constructors.

Saint Augustine had it: "The Abyss uttered its voice."

Harrow-on-the-Hill reminded the traveller, while the train shuddered at the platform, of the wonder of being somewhere accidental without having to move a muscle, without any requirement to step down and continue. Harrow, what he could see of it, the banal portrait in the frame of the window, was wrapped in servile homage around the long established, "next best" public school. Hopelessly large and inconvenient villas had expelled their post-colonial and City-based retirees and rentiers, in favour of a thriving culture of single rooms for single gentlemen in reduced circumstances, of hospices and terminal retreats serviced by nuns.

The voice! The voice from the bunker! I almost heard it. If, like the poet and performance artist B. Catling, I stored *everything*, all communications and inspirations, preliminary sketches and frames from favoured films, songs by Shirley Collins, on an obliging phone, then I would have called it up. I would have pumped away, as he did, with thick fingers, to unlock the key. That man's instincts were infallible. I had floated David Jones at him for years, without evident affinity being declared. Two men of South London who were poets and artists. Two men with family attachments and childhood visions in Rotherhithe. (Catling had somebody else, a hermit scholar on the island of Gozo, to do his Latin for him.) But my friend's engagement, absolute and for all time, came when, surfing his device, he happened across a recording of Jones reading from *The Anathemata*. "Piercing the eskered silt, discovering every stria, each score." The voice, the pitch, the cadence. Grand, yes. Fruity even. Confident and self-sustaining by production of resonance from within, when all else was in doubt and crumbling around him. The geese in the garden and the woman spurned (and spurning): all gone, made into art. The monastic cell of his retreat, visited by patrons and acolytes, heaped in a chaos of papers and tobacco tins, research and retreat, like the wartime hellhole, the rank private soldier's bothy moled out of a wet trench, duckboards and stinking boots. The comrades in arms whose absence thickens the atmosphere of the Harrow den with its heavy curtains and locked windows. But the jackets are tailored. The shirts are good. Catling plays the recording. This is the voice of an oracle. "Did he walk the water-lanes of the city from east of Bridge . . . Walking the nine river-fronting divisions of the city / of cities all."

Measured and marmoreal, the entirety of the reading was concluded before the train stirred. The living voice of the dead poet went out over a natural chain of three small hills, a spine running south towards River Brent, the Grand Union Canal, and the supposed location of the manmade conical mounds. Like Jones, I recited a consequence of given names—Harrow-on-the-Hill, Horsenden, Hanger Hill—in order to give some spurious veracity to my tale. In order to synthesise the witness of incorruptible things.

There was one student left, or so I took him to be, since he kept his head in a paperback book, and licked a yellow finger to turn the pages, breathing heavily and nodding in agreement with the author's sentiment. Together, we saw out the various Ruislip halts and the manors and meadows of Ickenham. Given his rejection of laptop, iPhone, Kindle, or other devices, in favour of a fistful of paper, I took him for an aspirant psychogeographer bound for Uxbridge and a walking seminar around the campus of Brunel University with Professor Self or Nick Papadimitriou, author of *Scarp*. Brunel was a set reminiscent of Truffaut's adaptation of *Fahrenheit 451*, where alienated cultists are made to behave like CGI projections brought to life. Before being released into motorway woods, where they recite memory recordings of favourite books. Old standards: Dickens, Defoe, Orwell, the Brontë women.

The reader had the carriage to himself. Stocking cap pulled low over his brow, gangsta fashion, misshapen knuckle rubbing nose at the conclusion of every paragraph, as if seeking permission to continue. I left him in solitary occupation. I was alone on the Hillingdon platform, one halt short of the terminal, always an unsatisfactory conclusion: a story junked before the murderer is revealed. Frozen for a few moments, taking my bearings, registering the modest harvest of surveillance cameras, the former waiting room shelter now designated PRIVATE, I noticed that the student, who had his back to the platform, cranked and twisted his neck, in order to stare straight at me and to hold up a thumb in a gesture of unwarranted brotherhood. I knew him but I couldn't give him a name or recall where we had met, communed, disputed, or attempted collaboration. He was so confident in his ownership of a purchased seat and in the spread of rucksack and Tupperware food cartons across the spaces on either side of him. If the glass had not separated us, he would have bumped elbows, squeezed a shoulder, or offered a culturally questionable high five. The youth was miming a sort of frenzied suicidal breaststroke as the train pulled slowly out. He held up the book he had been reading. It was one of my own, loose-leafed and broken in spine. I knew the title, but not much else: the object was as foreign to me now as the person still labouring to digest it, to improve my infelicities with smudgy revisions. With corrections so fierce they cut through the paper. My failure to identify this young man, more troubling with every yard walked away from the station, haunted the rest of the day's journey. Recognition, these days, was a lottery, even among my nearest and dearest.

My wife said that I walked right past her on the street, muttering and chewing.

"Be aware" warned the sign alerting me to the sponsored obscurity of the official Hillingdon maze map. "Be very aware." There is one of these "hidden in plain sight" productions at every London Underground station. "Be mindful of your surroundings. Don't get lost in contemplating the labyrinth, as in any city, there are thieves and pickpockets watching and waiting. If you have an iPhone, you can download a web app 'Labyrinth' to learn more about what it represents."

This struck me as an infinitely regressive system. The only passengers arriving on trains, while I made my own crude sketch of the labyrinth, in case it offered any clue to the location of the curious mounds photographed by Alba Zutique, were already eye-locked to their devices, rambling helplessly through the fractal pathways of cyberspace, or twisting skywards to assure themselves that every stolen image was preserved for ever in the billowing sock of a theoretical Cloud. They weren't in Hillingdon. They were barely in their own shoes. The public art map was of no interest. Somewhere, in a waiting room or an ambulance, they might luck on this labyrinth again, as they scrolled in panic, killing the boredom behind boredom, jolted into confrontation with their own mortality. Bumping over potholes, screaming for analgesics. Another hit of morphine. Comforted by strangers. By soldiers tasked with replacing nurses.

The labyrinth artwork has no connection to place. It is an over-inked portrait of a sagittal slice of brain matter, of fissures, nerves and parieto-occipital sulcus. And there are no obliging career thieves in Hillingdon, nothing as engaged or determined. The algorithmic labyrinth offers no mysteries. There is nothing to draw the pilgrim inwards. An X marks the spot where nobody is standing. At the centre is a smear of lipstick in an empty box. But if you zoom out, the formal pattern within the circle, within the rectangle, becomes a conical mound accessed by spiral paths. The labyrinth is a thumbprint, an identity badge. Once you let it into your iPhone, you are signed up, on a monthly debit: a seeker, a consumer, a client.

Orientated now, but unconvinced that I was advancing on the provisional target, and quite prepared to spend the day circling and doubling back on myself, I hung on to the acoustic footprints of the highway designated the A40. The tree screened road was shadowed by a parallel rail system that offered hope, should body or mind fail, of a return to my half-forgotten Hackney base. Already I was aware that I wasn't walking. The day was too comfortable. *I was writing.* And I was re-walking, even though, to the best of my knowledge, I had never been here before. I had no pre-composed texts from which to assemble livelier memories.

Smart coaches dominate this junction, boasting of their links with Oxford. Some species of "Green Way" or permitted footpath is suggested, but the chances of locating it, if I can get across the traffic to a teasing pavement, liable to be withdrawn for excavation and improvement at any moment, are slender. *Wait.* There is a silvered plaque, with fading honours, surviving from another era.

Striking out from such a relic—A40 LONG LANE JUNCTION MANAGEMENT OPENED BY STEVEN NORRIS MP, MINISTER FOR TRANSPORT LONDON, ON 17TH OCTOBER 1994, FOR THE HIGHWAYS AGENCY—you jolt. You travel through time. Another century, another millennium. Old gods and discontinued promises. The unpolished and weathered memorial, like a Victorian trade sign on the end wall of a Hoxton warehouse, speaks of motorway utopianism. It speaks of a sleek-suited political functionary recognised and promoted by that gap-year prime minister, John Major. Straight out of the car showroom, Norris was canny enough to play along with his gladhanding tabloid stereotype. Major, that frosted phantom, now looks, when set against the messianic conviction of the big picture figures on either side of him, a model of restraint and decency. His evident flaws, his sexual and careerist opportunism, and catastrophic over-promotion, have been forgiven and forgotten. A modest Eurocrat, a gentleman banker with a Dickensian backstory and ropey brother, Major is indulged because of his passion for cricket, for lazy days with other bankers and freeloaders at the Oval: a late-Orwellian in dirty times.

The plaque fades to Hillingdon oblivion, but the named minister thrives; rising, falling, rising again, rising further, boosted and shamed. "Politician and businessman", obituary tributes will proclaim, as if there were a real distinction between the twinned pathologies. Steve "Shagger" Norris, once of Hackney, before the ultimate wave of terminal gentrification broke, juggled many mistresses to advantage and managed to move on before the blade dropped. Major put him in charge of the Jubilee Line Extension, way ahead of its Olympic apotheosis, but in time to weigh up development opportunities useful for the next career adjustment. The Jubilee, back then, was the largest and loudest addition to the Underground network. Plot and plan your tunnels, make a deal for excavated soil, buy into dying zones where prosperity is assured by the promise of carrying City migrants, smoothly and swiftly, to somewhere else. To Canary Wharf and Liverpool Street. To Paddington and Heathrow.

Connected clusters of towers, connected to other identical clusters, were pillowed in dereliction, in despair, but rising above it. You are an investor in the future or you are nothing: a yard of urine puddled pavement and a polystyrene coffee cup where a few brown coins swim among the dregs. Shagger, when you examined the confident portrait above any of the enhanced CVs available at the flick of a screen, was the epitome of the neo-liberal soft right. The right to buy and buy again. The handshake in the buckled driving glove. The Man Who Would Be Mayor: standing twice, rejected twice. Runner-up to Ken Livingstone. A willing sub, coming off the bench when the popular novelist, Lord Archer, took a brief sabbatical in order to research conditions in Belmarsh Prison for a chart-topping autobiography of endurance and resurrection.

Norris faces his portraitists with suet smile and eyes disappearing into folds of complacent flesh. Confident hair aligns with a fat silk tie. He is an unacknowledged model for the Boris Johnson type: Oxford, of course, but achieved from a Liverpool grammar school. A hard worker and a networker: President of the University Law Society. Parliament by way of an Epping Forest by-election. Interests in the motor trade: showroom affable, shrewd and articulate, without any obvious convictions. Able to champion totally opposed factions at the same time: Chairman of the National Cycling Strategy Board *and* Director General of the Road Haulage association. Patron of charities. Pro-hanging and pioneer supporter of gay rights. Special interest in the age of consent. Cheerleader for Rudy Giuliani and his no-nonsense approach to street crime in New York City. Invites Giuliani Partners to advise him when he runs London. When his stock crashes, his shaggy-mopped avatar, Boris Johnson, becomes the favoured candidate. Johnson times his run to perfection: he is Norris through a tumble dryer. Shirt-tails flapping.

But Steve was ahead of the curve. Transport, infrastructure, property. In the post-Thatcher dreamworld, he was the epitome of enterprise. Launch the railway, mop up failed estates. Enclose Soho for a project without limits. Norris is chairman of Soho Estates. He controls sixty acres of the district. All that history! All those romantic pastry shops and drinking clubs. All the cutting rooms where pornographers bought into art. Norris and Boris. Norris as the visionary who actually did get it done. Boris as the public clown, the stooge who takes the fall. Steve chairs billion pound entertainment resorts in Kent: yes! He is Future-Build Limited, Proptech Construction: yes! He is a partner in Sanctuary Investments: yes! He sits on the board of Transport for London: yes! He sits on the main board of Cubic Corporation of San Diego, defence and transportation technology: yes, yes, yes! Extraordinary renditions of capital! He gets it done! Again. His smile is the smile of the honey bear. He is the operator linking everything. He masterminds motorway action and he gives out Prince Michael's International Road Safety Awards. He is a patron of the Urology Foundation and Chairman of Canal Sports. He holds an Honorary Doctorate of Law from the University of East London, out there where it is all about to kick off, where the Elizabeth Line meets ExCel Centre and where the City Airport overflies the magnificent sugar factory.

The self-made serial opportunist weeps immoderately at show tunes. He cruises the orbit of the M25, sniffing out development opportunities in his pea-green Roller, mainlining Liza Minnelli and Barbara Streisand, tears coursing down the interview pancake of the latest TV dust-over. He rides the Westway like the pope of all he surveys: the ten-storey rolling adverts, the mega hotels, the universities thinking up new honours to confer. He can take a joke. His leather-insulated chariot is self-parody. The Johnson trick. Boris and Norris. "I know more about London's bus and Tube network than almost anyone alive." The journalist Tim Adams called him "the Billy Graham of bus lanes; the Jimmy Swaggart of the Central Line". Criticism is brushed aside, it emanates from that "monstrous regiment of harpies". *Guardian*. Tofu. Woke.

The comedy tag Steve is finessing for his gravestone reads: "Here lies Steven Norris". Which is both unfair and untrue. He'll find some way to flog his ashes as landfill. A sense of humour covers all misdemeanours, every crime a boast. Leave that epitaph to Boris.

The Hillingdon plaque, fading away but still screwed firmly to London stock brick, is the best obituary. The marker from which our walk into madness must begin.

Freezeland Way is a training ground for bus drivers, probably initiated by Norris, with a semi-retired shopping precinct attached. The morning is now ripe with potential and I strike out, whistling, as if I were a reincarnation of Laurie Lee, waxing lyrical on the road to Spain. After a line of refuse trucks, I came on a stile, a wild copse rancid with incident and blue plastic shreds; English fields beyond, with the A40 a hissing snark at the event horizon. In an unblemished cerulean sky, smoky white contrails sketch their kamikaze dives somewhere over Greenford. I succumbed, pissed among thorns, careful to avoid the still steaming compost mat laid down by white van men, crapping while they chomped on burger cartons, still high and staggering on diesel fumes and the wood alcohol residue of vagrants, out here roaming these uncontested fringes.

It was tempting to follow a line trampled through grass, a potential path dressed with texture of animal hair, an admix of grey wool and barbed wire. Tempting but unwise. "Would we be let in Mister?" asks Beckett's Dublin child, "fidgeting at the gate". "Would we get out?" That is the treacherous voice of experience. "So on, derelict, as from a bush of gorse on fire." We wouldn't escape this false meadow, that is sure. This tease of pre-development wilderness, between road and permitted cycle track, has no business with travellers and pilgrims and the awkward ones who insist on butting through hedges, tearing flesh on barriers—but pushing on, idiotically, without map or machete. This land is under-narrated, biding its time, unfarmed, lacking cattle, but owned, remotely, and watched everywhere. You can shit but you can't stay.

Take the open road, baffle of trees on either side, big white arrow for direction of travel (back where you came from). Specks of grain like burnt rice set into the metallic blue of mildly cambered tarmac: life doesn't get any better, no cars, no bicycles, no speed walkers yakking as they sway on their Nordic poles. *Something has to be wrong.* Such an idyll, for certain temperaments, is freighted with threat. Detours are not an option. I try an opening in the woods, but the track succumbs to broken branches, tipped trees, a poisoned creek. And a fox trotting towards the tunnel beneath the motorway. Free passage for predators. No roadkill harvest for gleaners.

What could be better, vague quest, flat lands with no hint as yet of the mountains of madness? What could be more troubling? What price would have to be paid for this day's indulgence? Through a gap in the high guardian hedge, that cultivated rood screen of overgrown and self-propagated arboreal chaos, was a promising meadow. It was worth the damp trousers, soaking boots and knee-high tares, to make a close inspection of a set of sculptural interventions lined up like gallows designed for later-day highwaymen by a sadistic geometrician. Iron masts with a triangular arrangement from which it would be possible to suspend two victims at a time, at a respectful distance, one from the other. One facing west, one east: weather chimes. Or mutineers in the royal navy, roped to the yardarm, beneath the skeletal outline of a sail without canvas. No Landseer cattle. No tractors. No Millais peasants. Agriculture has been set aside in favour of these unexplained light poles.

There was a Hitchcockian moment, when, out of nowhere, a white jet plane, swooping low overhead, heard before seen, shadow before substance, explained the structures in the field. I was aligned with the flight path from Northolt Aerodrome, a site with its own triangles and sinister symbolism, on the north side of the A40. Lights blinked and warned, keeping the pilots a few feet above the trees.

A short distance along the still deserted, still inviting road, the inverted triangles of the lighting poles were flipped for the pointed roof of what I took to be a bird feeder disguised as an alpine chalet. On closer inspection, this reliquary proved to be a select library for pilgrims. It was connected in some way I could not divine with electrical and magnetic force fields, with the barely registered but headache-inducing pulses of white xenon flashers.

The books were an amenity. Take one, leave one in exchange. Tempting, until you started to examine what was on offer. Blockbusters, self-help manuals, morally improving fables for infants, nature cures, young adult fantasies for reluctant pensioners. My rucksack, at this early stage, was not troublesome, but it might be handy, before the day was much older, to leave the thousand-page heft of *City of God* and to go away with the slender print-on-demand version of the only book I had previously read, *At the Mountains of Madness* by H. P. Lovecraft. (This was another recommendation by Catling, on my first visit to his house alongside the Old Kent Road.) The title was fortuitous, a theme for my walk.

I finger-surfed the pristine pages and caught words that played right back, as part of the shockwave manufactured on the treadmill of traffic, to my encounter with the Norris plaque. To my morbid meditation on the political classes. On those cosmetically enhanced life forms with their strobing suits and rigid hair. Lovecraft's ultimate horror, buried deep beneath the Antarctic ice shelf, and conjured from echoes of Poe, was the "demonic Shoggoth". Slime-bucket monsters capable of wrenching decapitations. The very word "shoggoth" sounds like a drunk with a cleft palate trying to say "Shagger". Shoggoths are victims of their unrestrained lusts and blind impulses. But you can't blame them. It's their upbringing, environment, conditioning. They have been mastered and enslaved by colours out of space, by the market forces of Antarctic Darwinianism. They are the afterbirth of the moral mess when the aliens from distant star systems finally get it done. "Formless protoplasm able to mock and reflect all forms and organs and processes—viscous agglutinations of bubbling cells—rubbery . . . infinitely plastic and ductile—slaves of suggestion, builders of cities."

Adequately apprenticed to the idyll of the bucolic roadway corridor, cycle track and official footpath, screened from the angry reality of the A40 and its connections to Oxford and the west, Birmingham and the Midlands, the traveller was now qualified to be dumped, in the outermost grades of his highway initiation, on a strip of hard shoulder, pressed against the security of a tangled hedge. Now the fields with their invasive sculptural devices, warnings to low-flying aircraft, were the secrets.

Across twin traffic streams, and the vermin sanctuary of the central reservation, was a mirror world, also screened by a discretion of managed arboriculture. The urge towards the imperative of London, the only destination that mattered, bruised the burning air: they died, a little more each time, the ones returning from deeper England. And the beaten adventurers creeping home through "intersidereal space" from the "Outer Countries": Nueva York, Tokyorama, Florence, Beaconsfield, Berlin, Lancaster and Legoland.

And what was the implication, barely registered, of those inverted L-shaped lighting poles, like so many Allen keys for self-assembly furniture? Or sites of execution awaiting a round-up of dissidents. Allen keys, I remembered, had another name: hex. For the release of hexagonal screw heads. And for the prayers uttered, knuckles blooded, when fiddling some resistant chair into viable form. Hex is a spell, a curse. A warning. These stunted poles can curdle the milk in which flies drown. They cannot conjure visions of the conical mounds that must be somewhere in the vicinity. They alert the traveller to the imminence of Northolt Aerodrome, with its hexagonal casting of flight paths, its covert departures and arrivals.

Was it wise to continue? I consulted my Lovecraft.

"In the whole spectacle there was a persistent, pervasive hint of stupendous secrecy and potential revelation. It was as if these stark, nightmare spires marked the pylons of a frightful gateway into forbidden spheres of dream, and complex gulfs of remote time, space, and ultra-dimensionality. I could not help feeling that they were evil things—mountains of madness whose farther slopes looked out over some accursed ultimate abyss. That seething, half-luminous cloud background held ineffable suggestions of a vague, ethereal beyondness far more terrestrially spatial, and gave appalling reminders of the utter remoteness, separateness, desolation, and aeon-long death of this untrodden and unfathomed austral world."

Lovecraft can sound like a Highways Agency copywriter: "A vague, ethereal beyondness". Do we call up the language we require to justify the insanity of our futile expeditions? Or do these fragments seduce us into marking out an occulted miasma of signs and sigils, digitally sampled bites for future pilgrims? The pylons are present. As are the "gulfs". Lovecraft's delirious incantations freeze into a statement of the obvious a few yards beyond the modest perimeter fence with its charm bracelet of swivelling security cameras.

I lifted my camera to flatter a parade of frosted Gulfstream Aerospace jets, decorated with Arabic numerals. Their passenger doors were open, ready for immediate transit, flight plans undeclared to the usual authorities. Jaunts, social or political, to Caribbean tax shelters. To the Black Sea, Khartoum, Uzbekistan, Burkina Faso. And sub-orbital tourism to the Kármán Line, the duty-free border of infinite space. Given the right meteorological conditions, and payment in the approximate region of a banker's bonus, you can soar as far above Northolt as the distance, down here in the muck, up the redundant motorway to Wolverhampton. London looks a lot cleaner from the suburbs of space. You can see how the manmade mountains play against the sprawl of a choked and breathless metropolis.

Travel for those "seeking quick, discreet and secure departure" is a smooth affair, with a fifteen-mile limousine snooze from central London being the toughest part of the package. "Passengers are processed promptly through the MOD security gates before being directed to the airfield terminal entrance to be met and greeted by experienced and friendly staff from Universal Weather Aviation." Extraordinary rendition comes with "executive lounge, complimentary food and drink". And personalised market updates from this week's Chancellor of the Exchequer.

It should not be forgotten that Northolt is still an operative RAF station, used and abused by our transatlantic masters. Some flights come with non-optional handcuffs and black bags over the head. Some flights render dead royals to London. Princess Diana, autopsied, was returned from Paris. Queen Elizabeth II from Balmoral. There would be stamping and drummed processions of uniformed mourners following flower-draped hearses along emptied country roads to nominated castles. To sanctified burial sites with descending elevators. Discreet blanket coverage would hide inconvenient attendees, black sheep of the extended royal family, serial misspeakers. The country would pause, some loyal citizens shuffling through the night to witness the crowned box on its catafalque, some to stare transfixed at a huge screen. We learn in these times to appreciate the poetry of slow cinema. Everything smells of horseshit, cut flowers and cellophane.

Caught on barbed wire, like a blind crow sucked in by the unexpected roar and detonation of a jet engine, I spooled back to memory footage of another funeral: the dead queen's dead father, a committed smoker, and the nation's grieving in 1952. That was before colour happened. And when flights were still dreams. It rained, always, as part of state ceremony. At Christmas, power lines would be down and we would gather in the dark, licking the puckered skins of rare and imported oranges, too precious to peel. We came as a duty to London, through shuddering tunnels and smoke, to join the expectant crowds camped out to witness the dawn of this second Elizabethan age. Sodden, we dragged ourselves underground, into a rank animal heat, before surfacing somewhere near the centre, where flocks of respectably presented amateur prostitutes, umbrellas furled despite the downpour, offered intimate acquaintance, brisk servicing by hand or loins, to regiments of bedazzled provincials. It was never true that Londoners were in a rush and unapproachable. Under the dirt and the post-war psychosis this was a safe city. A uniformed bobby, protector-pimp to these obliging ladies, on every Soho corner.

To be exposed, as a child with only an illustrated sense of the founding myths of our island's story, to the great monochrome newsreel of undeniable actuality, was a significant rite of passage. And, as part of the exercise, my father brought us out to Northolt. That day came back to me now. Draughty sheds. A plane that had seen service and smelt of it, rubbery, metal fatigued with exposed ribs. A London shaking off the tremors of blitz. Going up, propellers hammering, fuselage creaking, deaf and not daring to blink, gripping hard arm rests, the experience was more a test of nerve than a pleasure circuit of airstrip and northwest suburbs. There were no mounds, no pyramids. The flight was not about going anywhere. It was about returning from Paddington to Wales and saying that we had been up in the clouds over London. We did not identify Buckingham Palace or Tower Bridge, but we caught a skewed glimpse of Ruislip Lido and Milton's Cottage in Chalfont St. Giles.

My reverie faded when I trod on something that squelched. The path ahead, for this whole stretch, directly across the road from the aerodrome, was straight and clear and true. It was blessed with a carpet of hundreds of crab apples that nobody wanted to pick. And other fatter and greener apples like the windfall of Kentish orchards. Animals spurned this bounty. Unbitten, innocent of worms, the apples rolled with the shaking of the road, the revolution of our bulging globe. They formed two quite distinct ridges, with a still life scatter where the fruit had been kicked by other pilgrims. There were no fruit trees in the thatch of the hedge. The apples might have belonged to a shunted lorry. They were well away from tarmac. They challenged the allocated pedestrian path. A bridal train of metaphors leading towards the persistent rumour of the mounds.

After the apples, the way cleared; names recollected from the instructional text books of childhood attached themselves to the plants and weeds of the wayside. Teasel, toadflex, honeysuckle, field scabious: all present and correct before my route was abruptly discontinued at a major junction, a road slashing down from Ruislip. Now I could feel the massive displacement of the mounds, but I could not see them. They must be very close, a few hundred yards, at the most, from where I was halted, stymied, my hiking permit revoked.

Forced inland, the footpath having turned into a slithery exit ramp, into designated hard shoulder, a killing field for badgers and foxes, and having nothing to draw on beyond Alba Zutique's photographs of photographs, mounds that could have started life in Athens or Paris, and teasing prompts from Lovecraft, who had already completed the story I was trying to assemble, the country became as unyielding as a translation of a familiar poem into an unfamiliar language. Nothing could be achieved until the mounds were conquered: truth was hiding on the far side of expectation. "The ultimate, nameless thing beyond the mountains of madness," Lovecraft wrote.

The sudden bereavement of the absence of apples was unmanning. But there had been something odd and outside nature in this late-season harvest alongside the A40: *there were no flies.* Fallen fruit, winded and bruised, skin broken, was the delight, the sustenance of fruit flies in suburban gardens. They licked and sucked. Cultellus fangs honed like blades. They shared a genetic inheritance with those oversize creatures, strange mammals who planted trees but allowed fruit to lie untouched on the ground. Some of the woken flies, in the delirious drench of rot, remembered earlier lives. Modest transfusions of human blood, exposed veins in the necks of restless and tossing sleepers. Naked shoulders, moist armpits, pyjamas gaping over groins. The fever of their brief cycle of mortality. The flies scraped, drank and sang. They sought the shadows.

What unbalanced this coming away from the steady flow of traffic, from the waiting aircraft, was the realisation that independent movement was anachronistic, a by-product of time travel. Out on our radial and orbital motorways, there was no reliable movement. Righteous protestors, advocates of unrestrained nature, rose early to swarm over bridges, to invade tunnels, to paste themselves to tarmac. Later, when the great galleries sponsored by oil interests opened to the public, they would hurl cans of tomato soup— Warhol irony—at paintings by Vincent van Gogh. Or at the monumental apples of Paul Cezanne, after he had his acute accent amputated, for reasons of authenticity, on his way to exhibition in a former power station on the banks of the Thames. All patrons were suspect. Nobody gives money away with a pure heart. Killing fumes, coughed from miles of stalled traffic, formed a cloud over estates and golf courses.

Van Gogh walked London, walked the borders of parks, the graphic outline of mounds still to be constructed.

He walked in anguish and ecstasy from Isleworth, under another flight path, to the City of bankers, the shops of dealers in prints. Not yet mad enough to paint, Vincent poured his pain into letters. He stormed the suburbs.

Undecided whether to carry on, to force a passage, or to return, whatever the risk, to the security of the A40, I stared at the triumphal arch of the Shree Kutch Leva Patel Community (UK). But did I qualify? There were sacred cows and gods and peacocks, flags and inviting avenues beyond the locked gates and the CCTV warnings. The temples established themselves here after Kenya's independence and Idi Amin's expulsion of successful Asian business operatives and entrepreneurs. Willesden, Golders Green, Harrow, Woolwich: they purchased ground and built their places of worship and community activity in London's suburbs. The children of immigrants are schooled in languages of home, in Gujarati. They are tutored in mathematics and physics. There is a day centre for senior citizens almost as old as myself. And for those who have better things to do than tramp the fringes of airports and reservoirs, taking guidance from the books of deranged solitaries in musty New England rooms.

I need one of my angels. I'm tempted to charge off to where I know the mountains *should* be, straight through the labyrinth of a new estate that surely won't be here whenever, if ever, I return. But like Beckett's urchin, outside the field where a hurling engagement is happening, I know how it works. "I was in that field before and I got put out." Cul-de-sacs are unforgiving. Cycling routes, like the freedom paths for moles and badgers, have their overpasses and tunnels. Walkers are suspect. If the estate is upmarket, on a hill in Surrey, there will be patrol cars. Out here, there is meaningful silence and the yelping of pre-recorded curs. Old ladies, more often than not, emerge in woodland, on wild coast paths, on the lip of a terrifying chasm to which they could never have walked. My wife remarks on it. She calls them "*your* old ladies". They manifest when most needed, putting us straight by telling us to go back the way we have come and to try again on another day. They might offer a boiled sweet, and the quick grin of a cat, a flick of tongue between dry lips.

There is one of the species, fifty or sixty yards ahead, taking her rest in the imagined shade of a ruined and roofless bus shelter. She looks something like a grandmother who decided, eighty years ago, not to indulge in children. But I have to ask. There is no other human visible in the entire panorama of hyper-normal weirdness.

"Do you know—excuse me, please—where I can find the mounds? The pyramids? Somewhere close to the A40?"

She hisses, punctured by the outrage. This is not a face, it's a bone mask. Out of Greek tragedy. And there is another one under it, under the congealed paint and the lacquered fixative, under the sticky lashes like flea combs. The old lady is respectable, still mobile, stickless but propped against the shattered cobweb in the panel of unbreakable glass. She is envenomed, a retired Medea of the Metropolitan Line. She twists her neck, as if to summon the bus that no longer tends this route.

"Certainly not! *Here on West End Road?* Never! Not at all."

Behind her was a stalking beast from the Mesozoic with dorsal scutes and dermal armour. This ankylosaurid, a full-sized, dull green pinacosaurus, sex undetermined, tramped the line of a shallow irrigation canal, enraptured by glimpses of its own reflection in the scummy water. It had been chosen, by remote investors, as the ideal beast to guard the suspiciously verdant boundaries of a Floodlit Driving Range, a chunk of real estate dedicated to the American Way. *Love golf? Love London. With coffee shop and licensed bar.* You could hear the whip of beta titanium drivers parting the air and the arcs they described as they sent balls swirling through space in the general direction of Greenford, huddled and safe, 3,100 yards in the distance. There was life out there, bunkered beyond sand traps and earthworks.

I couldn't see the putting greens or the parked Range Rovers of active recreationalists. The ditch and the low fence seemed to enclose a zoo of stalled creatures, gathered in one place, but divided by several million years, in a suburban rip-off of *Jurassic Park*.

It was enough to send me scuttling blind across the A4180, a death strip blitzed with traffic released by stop lights for road works that must have been happening somewhere else. Perhaps, after all, undone by apples, I had missed the mounds in my dumb adherence to the old straight track. Beyond the security mesh, there was a promising hint of elevation, of foothill, no less attractive for the remote crump of gunfire. The crackling and irregular potshots of rat hunters or destroyers of clay pigeons. I spotted a young Sikh man coming down the slope. He was today's messenger of fate, courteous and precise. I'm sure he walked this route, season by season, ready to impart secret knowledge to those who knew when and how to ask.

"The mountains? About half an hour."

Like a true pilgrim, he measured distance by time.

"To the big roundabout, then left on Church Road."

And now, miraculously, everything unfolded, precisely as the Sikh foretold. Coming into occupied territory, the concept of the mounds was domesticated. The people were Asian or Polish, with a smattering of Africans moving towards a strip of functioning shops. This was a better London, offering services, and spreading out to fill the lacuna between twinned airports, Heathrow and Northolt.

The largest signs pointed travellers in the general direction of the Polish War Memorial on the edge of Western Avenue. My spirits revived, I was prepared for whatever challenges lay ahead. The ultimate building in the precinct announced itself—what else?—as DREAM CAFÉ (TAKE AWAY OR EAT IN). Shining windows promised all-day breakfasts, produced to order, in any combination, by a solid man in an apron. An immaculate oasis. Open to all. Dream on.

Warmly welcomed, order taken by Polish proprietor and passed across to an attentive but non-obsequious waiting woman straight out of Kafka's *Castle* troop, I settled at my kitchen-facing Formica table, to await the promised arrival of the feast, a quality plate preceded by a clean mug of the best coffee. Dreamtime indeed. The man in the apron, showing no alarm at my enquiry, confirmed that the holy mountains were situated right at the end of this miraculously ordinary street.

"You cannot cross over until you find the library. There is a fine and resolute walk beneath the linden trees."

Library? Trees? This was the place. And more than that, as I turned away from the counter, I caught a glimpse of the person at the table by the window; another solitary, sharing this scrubbed and serviced Polish diner with two African women and a man in a blue boiler suit emblazoned with a dozen security logos.

"John?"

The man turned, a crisp bacon tongue suspended from his fork, a few streaks of the runny egg filtering through the rust of his beard. By one of those coincidences that happen in life, but carry no conviction in works of fiction, I had chosen the same café, at the same hour, as one of my former collaborators, a peripatetic filmmaker who was in danger of giving selfies a good name. John Rogers.

The Man of Essex perambulated on a weekly basis, branching out and away from his base in Leytonstone. Like me, he was sensitive to the tremors currently emanating out of Northolt. On film, John talked to himself, quietly, steadily, without appearing eccentric or screaming "awesome!" at regular intervals. Where necessary, he even confessed his ignorance, as he put in the hard miles, musing and amusing, action captured by the camera on a stick.

This was a seasonal pilgrimage for Rogers, a return of sorts. The possibilities of London are never exhausted, he said, but it is always good to come back at them from a different direction. John sought the mountain and the mountain sought its witness. How the Rogers pitch worked, its special charm, was in the presentation of a version of London that was better than tired reality. The documentarian reached out towards a pagan past, ancestors waiting on the instruction of the stars. Even the whims of developers could be incorporated into his Situationist map of the good life.

"That white arch over Wembley Stadium, coming down here today, it really caught my eye. But I was hoping for a rainbow."

These quasi-biblical manifestations, bent light teased by water droplets, had become an electromagnetic commonplace accompanying every stage of the slow-drip release of news about the latest royal death; programmed to appear on cue for the cameras, over Windsor Castle, doubled into significance over marchers and mourners. Fair and foul, the weather behaved appropriately.

John confessed that he was a little feverish in the head, sickened by the usual non-specific consequences of city life, even in Leytonstone, where regular commutes were a necessary condition of engagement. Playing Hamlet to his selfie stick, he diagnosed his present state as: "worn out", "cooked", "a bit leggy". His legs were not the problem. The difficulty lay somewhere between lungs and load. The smile never drooped. He marched with his mechanical conscience, never judging, all hearing, and he did not repine. As a familiar of High Beach, the Epping Forest trails, and ruinous interventions along the Lea Valley, John said that he found these far western lands somewhat "uncanny". What he knew of the mounds spoke of "Satanic rituals and magick with a 'k', Crowleyite séances".

Therefore, he topped up his brimming mug. He sipped. He made his notes, in case he should, one day, convert his research into a proper book. His working library was not a shed buried under pamphlets, but the open road. Celebrate whatever you find, leave something in exchange. Barter and accident. Guidance by a distant hand parting the clouds. Instruction from those who had once tramped the same turf. "Wildness. Refusal. Illumination," said Raymond Lull's wheel of fate, a set of overlapping plastic disks he kept in a pocket of his rucksack, in order to forecast the outcome of the latest excursion. "Spontaneous bibliomancy," they call it. Confirmation in other voices of the road already taken. The neurosis of the gambler: Russian roulette with a bullet in every chamber.

Stichomancy is the counting of lines "in books taken at hazard". Or reading a laminated menu, Polish-English, upside down. And we are guilty of all these quirks. *Rhapsodomany* is chanting misquoted verses as you tramp. The book that is picked by the guided hand, from however limited a supply, is believed to hold the truth. But there is betrayal too. The chosen volume will tend to open at a passage favoured by some previous owner. You find what you want to need. Not truth, but something kinder: the postponement of hope.

One mystery was solved: it was John Rogers who left the Lovecraft in the wayside shrine, on the path from Hillingdon. And in exchange he had acquired *Faux Mountains* by Michael Jakob. It felt like a more accurate and subtler key to his search. The mounds of Northolt were unnatural. They were true fakes, spirit traps.

Asking me to hold his camera high, he read aloud:

"Moving debris to the outskirts of the city, out of sight, already allowed during the immense construction site, which lasted a quarter of a century, to forget the ruinous state of the post-war landscape . . . Natural camouflage completed the displacement by offering visitors a landscape of great banality.

"One of the effects of this strategy of evacuation and occultation is the topographical non-relation between the artificial mountains and the city they 'crowned', without it really mattering to the later . . . The artificial mounds were prominent, but they had nothing to say.

"By piling up words, the artist is forced to descend into the 'mountains' of language, where each word contains crevices and reveals one subterranean stratum after another."

A person of charm, recognising another of similar dispensation, Rogers invited the waitress to read the last paragraph in her lovely voice, hesitating over "crevices" and "subterranean stratum". He thought, in the edit, this would give him something extra.

Replete, cheered by human exchanges, memories shared between one of the African women and the Polish cook, who never needed to set down his frying pan, we paid and left. The owner wished us well and hoped that we would return, to become irregular regulars with our own reserved mugs and tables.

Now as we struck north, it was a going forward. Everything was new. A stiff flag attached to a lighting pole, with script bold enough to catch the eyes of motorists held in a perpetual jam, warned: VISIONS FOR NORTHOLT. We studied the street, alerted to potential sightings of other pilgrims. Surviving royals, however young, however spurned, however broken, had crept with their marshals and courtiers, behind the boxed corpse of the long-lived queen, all the way to Windsor; so pinched and glazed they appeared. It was as if they were witnessing their own predicted end, by media rape or guillotine. Republicanism stood off, somewhere remote, as yet, behind a witnessing horse with an empty saddle. At the shadowline.

Like the mourners, we advanced shoulder to shoulder in private reverie, thinking of supper and the fireside. In mesmerised lockstep. We looked for other walkers, known and unknown. Those with an allegiance to the great theme, also heading, on this very morning, for the fabled mounds. We listed London spirits still on the loose. Nick Papadimitriou, by these streams and roads, close-invigilating vegetation, sleeping in sheds and water towers, carrying evidence home. Stephen Watts, the poet of poets, rising daily to his invariable task, following rivers, in converse with all those whose lives brushed his own. He spoke of inhabiting a place that was not "just a recess from which the anabasis came". Referencing a march from coast to interior by Cyrus the Younger, Stephen vowed to do the same, both ways. He was tough as only a poet can be on speech and the causes of speech. He never failed to draw breath at the right stopping place, midway on life's journey. He considered processions and royal progresses and the swollen regiment of the returning dead, in verses he titled "Funeral Procession for Queen Eleanor". "I've sculpted them at the meadow's edge, / endless columns for the arched blue sky. / Though we do not believe in monarchies, / though we must live in a republic of dogs.

/ The tired & dancing column on the road / has risen and rotated in its creamy void."

The column advances. Life had undone so many. The outliers of the outer zones threatened to overwhelm sleepwalking conformists. It was a miracle that we didn't, this very day, trample on the toes of other seekers. Chris McCabe was somewhere obscure, digging through unquiet sleepers in the ring of cemeteries, calling them back to heat and voice. Alba Zutique was casting her mental projections, heaping up a spoil of archive, prints of prints, sketching the outline of the humpback mounds for which we were still searching.

There was no logistic help in the new library. The custodian, perfectly civil, informed me that they kept no maps or volumes of local history. Such matters have been discontinued, stretched budgets do not run to special interests. Never leaving his workstation and the folded pamphlets available to those in need, he knew nothing about mountains. The neighbouring park, Northala Fields, could, if I was interested in pursuing the matter, be called up on a computer screen. Phones rang. Devices bleeped. Supplicants sneezed and waited their turn. Fat blockbuster novels were sweating unviolated in their prophylactic sheaths, sticking fast, one to the next, impossible to extract. Lighting was dim. Heating was left to the spectral glow of the waiting screens. No students came in from the street. Nobody asked after mountains.

Afternoon light flinched and bent against the pull of alluvium and recently modified ground. Clouds were costive with fathoms of unshed water. John muzzled the irritating inquisition of his camera. It was done. And, as the day lost conviction, domestic duties hauled him in. There were voices in his ear inviting him to return down the Central

Line from Northolt, carrying back the digital record of his adventures, securely stored. All those unfilmed miles to Leytonstone were nothing without the little red light. They never happened. What a run! Stopping and starting. Pausing without explanation. Visions glimpsed and then withdrawn. If he tried to register the blue-remembered mounds, they would fade into an overloaded sky. If the camera was reactivated from the window of his carriage, stacked earth would lose its material form and become another useless metaphor. He would be plagiarising Alba Zutique.

"She did nothing, she trembled at the sight of the mountains."

That was another book he had sampled and left behind. A smart young woman, French, imagined the mother of Beckett at her widow's window, "devouring the outdoors". That novel buzzed along without a false note, a purgative against the flatus of verbiage. "Always on the road. *The prison of memory*."

John came to the crossing, the edge of the path, the official Northala signboard, then he struck off, directly, on the short route to the station. If you quit at the right moment, there is always a way out. Insist on a fool's quest and you'll suffer for it. The thesis of *Faux Mountains* was persuasive.

The map on the board warned against starting fires for unsanctioned barbecues. And against motorcycles, detritus of picnics, unleashed curs. And offered, in exchange for obedience, a chain of immaculate mounds, breastplates for Amazons with four breasts. The tallest mound was accessible by way of a spiral path. That was the civic promise. Reality challenged it.

The question was: how could this sculpted massif, so enticing when glimpsed from a car speeding towards

Oxford, be so tricky to locate on foot? So hidden, so discreet, that even those who lived within a few hundred yards, denied all knowledge of these fields, these four fraternal mounds or mountlets.

Strolling believers felt like a natural outflow of the Shree Kutch Leva Community and the other temples around the western suburbs, communities translating faith and festival into ribbon development. An evening saunter had the atmosphere of a holy pilgrimage; parents with children, lovers with lovers, old men puffing slowly around the proscribed spiral to enlightenment.

The only authentic work person, attached to park or padlocked recreation centre, was tinkering with the exposed engine of his Land Rover, a necessary vehicle for covering the few yards between mounds, ponds and council bothy.

"Can you tell me anything about these mounds? Who built them, for example, and when?"

He does not lift his head. There is an angry suppurating boil standing proud on the third fold of his neck. "Mounds?"

The first, or nearest to the park entrance, nearest to the occupied mechanic, is a scantily clad molehill believing itself to be, by right, a mountain. It feels more like a summary test for altitude sickness in Peru than a rewilded Northolt slagheap. The traveller registers a beaten-down path leading upwards in a straight line, without a single recreationalist following the hint.

I climb. At a pitiful lurching scramble. Hands and knees.

In triumph, I make a sweep of road and copse, housing estates and aerodrome, knowing that looking back has consequences. From the aureole of the summit, an invaginated nipple, the only legitimate direction is east to the mirage of London. And east to the Great Matron,

Earth Mother: the queen mound of Northala with its spiral
pathway. While I weigh up my lack of options, I consider
the implications of the research already undertaken by
John Rogers. This mound complex, referencing Los
Guachimontones in style, Cairo and Berlin in its proximity
to the city, was rapidly assembled in a few years, starting
in 2004, from the rubble and dust of the imperious old
Wembley Stadium. The buried howls of national triumph
and disaster. The chants and expletives of the mob. And the
surface muck scraped away from inconvenient enterprises
between Shepherds Bush and Ballard's much loved
Westway ramp, that portal to the retro-futurism of the
Westfield shopping city. The declared cost was a modest
£5.5 million. Excavation into elevation. Developers were
charged £70/£90 for each lorryload of spoil. Convoys
rumbled a short distance, appeasing the Green lobby and
funding the creation of a nicely sculpted baffle, to shield
ratepayers of Northolt and Greenford from the perpetual
scream of the A40. Crushed and torn structures, shored up
by gabions, became cages of pulverised concrete preventing
the mound's gradual deflation.

The holy mountain, once the centre of a mappa mundi
of the New Jerusalem, was now exiled to the final fold
of the chart. My battered and much travelled *London
Street Atlas*, put out by Nicholson in 1993, yielded to the
unknown just beyond the Hangar Lane gyratory system
and the Guinness Brewery. Dated but timeless, the chain
of four Northala hillocks, viewing platforms, sky stations,
had the mysterious potency of things outside memory.
White folk, seduced into blind faith in the exclusive virtues
and privileges of their obscure island, did not see the
mounds. Believers in older gods perambulated, offering
a greeting to those encountered as they attempted the
impossibly slow spiral to the summit. A purged dialectic of

destruction created mountains in negative from the spoil of the ravished earth.

"Totenhain", the Germans called it. A grove of death. Funerary rafts for forgotten heroes. The evidence of war, cities in ruins, slaughtered citizens: all landscaped to hide the crime. Beyond dying industrial sites are markers for the end of activity.

In the hour of fate, world in balance, dimensions insecure, ground heated and pulsing, I reached the flattened summit of the highest mound. But I had cheated. I gave up on the spiral path—which felt more like a set of hoops, tight bands never ascending, no completed circuit leading upwards into another. Contour lines were manifest but they never touched. On these paths the damned were not in evidence. Nothing so glamorous. I scanned in vain for spectres of Norris and Boris, for the malign fiesta of other self-serving politicians, the bribed and the bribing, the loveless adulterers, the bearers of false witness drowning in tubs of their own shit. I dragged myself over the barrier of the gabions, skinning my knuckles to the bone, before clutching at handfuls of meagre grass.

There is always a messenger of sorts waiting. This one had his back to me. He was facing Northolt Aerodrome and screaming. He seemed to be calling down the circling aircraft. Jet engines roared. The adept had the orange jacket of an engineer. But I was quite mistaken. Sad karst of terrain struggling to live up to the illusion of progress. Shrouded in hood of office, the hireling groundsman was vaping smoke against the encroaching mist of evening, the hour of his release from the indolence of duty. He toyed with a radio-controlled device that sent a grass-gouging machine back and forth between the smoothed paths of the spiral ascent. The thing was not especially effective, but it did great noise. And it kept off the crows. It was the robot beast that roared and not the man. He was folded in on himself, lost in steam, electively mute. An extension of the park furniture.

Questions were futile. There was no oracle here beyond the sweeping panoramic view, if view was what you wanted. A schematic metal plan, like an instrument panel ripped from a crashed helicopter, listed the main attractions. Manmade stripes of energy, shaved into the grass, ran up and over the final mound and on towards the stumps and towers of enterprise on the distant horizon.

They flew the tragic body of the mangled "People's Princess" back from the Paris underpass, down the Thames, to Northolt. They flew the halted nonagenarian Queen Elizabeth II, for whom handshakes with two hapless Tory prime ministers in one day proved too much, back from Edinburgh. Was it, I wanted to ask the dope smoking gardener, a thick-shouldered man who might have doubled as a gravedigger, even remotely possible that these mounds were the covert site of royal burials? Our pyramids. Protocols, easily enforced by high walls and armed security, blacked out the usual chirpy news channels, in favour of static shots of iron Balmoral gates opening to let in suspicious vans. Or tourists gulling around palace perimeters, turning their phones on one another. Could the carriers of divine right, god's anointed, monarchs and virgin brides, have been quietly ferried across the A40, wheeled through fox tunnels, to the already prepared mounds? That would give them some purpose.

When they excavated Silbury Hill, to revive the spurious legend of a mounted horseman, a golden crown, a legendary Wessex chieftain, they found nothing. They say that Silbury was heaped up 2,500 years ago, a blink or two, in geological time, before the A4, but an authentic beacon, for sure, in anticipation of the coming highway.

And in anticipation too of that moment in Chris Petit's *Radio On*, when the psychotic squaddie, back from the terror of Northern Ireland, exits the car with trauma intact. They were asking the wrong question. Digging the wrong tunnels. As above, so below. Mine shafts, surgical strikes through the ribs of the stepped hill, were intrusive and flawed. Was the mound a maker of shadows, a sundial?

"Perhaps such momentous works," said Jacquetta Hawkes, "are only created when human imagination is unbalanced." E. O. Gordon, contemplating the ancient mounds that defined her cranky Christian-pagan energy map of London, wrote: "The circles of Abury (or Avebury) and Stonehenge and the vast earth-mound of Silbury Hill have been called the 'British Pyramids', from their astronomical construction, and because, like the Pyramids of Egypt, they are surrounded by the tombs of kings."

In his provocative set of "Appendices" to Gordon's survey, the Rev. John Griffith, "Interpreter of the Phaestus Disc-Calender", discourses on "facts of measurement" leading to "reasonable deductions". Calculations, hunches, proofs and equations: the Celtic man of the cloth is on the cusp of cracking the General Theory of Everything. Nudged by invisible masters, he moves from the stellar harvest of the heavens to Knossos, and from maze to mound, from Glastonbury to Silbury, to London. His wildest improvisations have a rind of unsubstantiated tradition. Griffith is conservative in his loyalties. The angle of the rising of Sirius at Avebury, three thousand years ago, "corresponds", so he says, to a Welsh legend: the decapitation of the blessed giant, Brân, and that timeless time when he ordered his followers to carry his head "to the White Mount, in London". Eyes open, the mantic caput would be buried at Tower Hill, facing France. And repelling invaders.

Studying his chart of the London Mounds, Griffith concluded that the Brân legend is "largely astronomical". He noticed, a century before Northala and the Northolt renditions, that Windsor Castle was part of a significant alignment: it anchored an equilateral triangle with Salt Hill and Stanmore.

Now, at the summit of the Mother Mound, the priest's thesis is laid out for our inspection. But Griffith is not done yet. "Mounds and straight roads should be studied together," he says. "Signal stations preceded long straight roads. And the mound-builders were the pioneers of road-makers. The positions of mounds, individually and relatively, were determined by astronomical requirements. The astronomy of the mounds is now duplicated in related roads." And more than this, the Welshman confesses that these mysteries were unravelled by way of a cheap protractor, "a shilling four-miles-to-an-inch Ordnance sheet", and contemplation of a new railway linking Rhondda and Swansea Bay. The man had pre-composed, in every respect, my own doomed expedition.

In my headlong descent—the same recklessly direct route as the climb—it felt as if every step might be the last. A boundary had been crossed and a taboo broken. The heavy clouds in their procession towards Windsor were stalling somewhere over Wormwood Scrubs. The balance between allegory and actuality was shot. No going back. Blood sang in the ears. My tongue stuck to the roof of the mouth. Chalky lumps in the palm of the hand congealed into a tightening string. Gasping for breath, I followed the trodden track in a cloud of unknowing; a drift of raised dust like a sudden rush of phantom bullocks. I traced the fraudulent ley line to the broad base of this fourth and final mound. Enough. No more prophets. No borough engineers. Animal instinct solicited a lap of water.

There was another man, an official allowed to leave his pickup truck within the precincts of the park, hiding in the evening shadows of the mother mound.

"Am I alright for the Grand Union?"

Unzipped, concentrating on his fist screen until his eyes bulged, the entitled one glared, concentration disturbed.

"Never heard of it."

The rage of necessity drove me on through a clinging thatch of woodland to the limits of this haunted park, where, losing the old straight track, I slithered down a mud slope to the canal. The Grand Union! A waterway lacking traffic and faithful horses.

"You have to cross at the bridge," said a massive crossbreed sharpening his claws on the bark of an oak. The beast was ventriloquised by a man in green camouflage, a woodland survivalist, in balaclava and dark glasses, hiding behind the gnarled trunk.

"Down, Virgil," the urban guerrilla commanded. As the animal clawed at the ground, torn between humping my leg or chewing it off. "He's only a puppy. He won't bite. Unless you provoke him."

"Which way for Paddington?"

"You got it all wrong, mate. Makes no sense. Turn right round. Climb up the road. Over the bridge. Then drop back down. Makes no odds, whichever way. Paddington or Slough."

The country was kind. A useful signpost advertised the estimated distance to Paddington, the great western rail hub: eight miles. As the crow flaps? Or traveller tramps, not yet leggy, but beginning to dissociate? Blood on old socks. After the mountains of madness, he was sentimental for home, the house for which he had lost the key. He had also mislaid, somewhere between Wembley Park and

Ruislip Manor, his grammatical status. No longer "I", but a shambling third person singular. A stranger seen from outside. The far bank, unreachable, with no sanctioned footpath, was kinder still. It was a picture not a place. A painting from another period. Meadows, playing fields, hills. He looked for sheep or goats. There were none. No milkmaids. No fisherfolk with rods and baskets.

Tender prospects, unpolluted by written accounts, but dull. He marched. A steady regular tread, without those necessary swerves to avoid cyclists who did not venture out so far. Or joggers who mobbed the tighter paths and competitive pavements of Hackney. His feet had swollen. They throbbed and rubbed against unyielding leather. No other pedestrians. He stepped it out, good English yards. An hour must have passed. There came a point of access to some riparian settlement and another sign: seven-and-three-quarter miles to Paddington. If he ran full throttle, until he retched, hands on knees, a fartlek jog, for one more hour, it would be nine miles. The old assumptions of space-time were derailed. The faster he thought he moved, the less ground he covered. Chased by a hellhound from the pit the traveller would be still as a statue.

Staying loyal to your designated path comes with a price. "Stories of others that your memory regurgitates." In Perivale or Alperton, this pilgrim is that frightful Lovecraftian other. Another other—with your face. He reads too much. He will go blind. If it is not in the book already, he is lost. Maps are lies. Signposts mock. The man, unauthored, is sweating now towards cardiac arrest, on a speeding conveyor belt running against a mounting charge sheet of wasted seconds. They are rolling up the scenery, and it has such charm, places you never glimpse from car or even train: too fast, too furious. If he had a sandwich left he would stop, chew, pick his teeth, reconsider. Watch the unflowing water. He would notice another carpet of crab apples climbing back to the tree.

And if he has to be here, before he can write it, or here again after the words are safely lodged on the page, then the other others will walk right through him without a nod of acknowledgement. Some he recognises. There are three of them, adepts of the old way, professional wordsmiths, hikers making their reports against the enforced plurality of the moment. He knows the books, but not the men, not really, not in three dimensions, let alone four. They are heading—he has read that story several times in separate accounts—to the airport. The long way round. Long enough to argue the toss. Academics, authors, nightwalkers. They can't wait to shake each other off, to get back to their moleskin notebooks, their laptops, their portable typewriters. Their silent houses in silent streets.

When the traveller had hopped and dragged for another hour and when a few figures, Indians, South Asians, began to appear, along with occupied narrowboats, folksy crafts, tarot cards, wood smoke, the three men came at him again, two in a line, one dropping back to scribble a prompt in his secret diary. The leader, burdened by a coat of many pockets, all he would need for his transatlantic voyage, was impatient. He had a specific destination and a specific time. The others slipstreamed. *And now my Northolt acquaintance was with them*: John Rogers and his friendly camera gathering footage without interrupting the feisty exchanges of the three unwise men.

As the traveller closed on canalside sections with which he had once been familiar—smouldering industries, offensive walls, an improvised yurt with hookah pipe, couch and rudimentary stove—he encountered the three questing walkers, heading out, on terms, fresher, sprightlier, more in accord. As his own tramp moved to a conclusion, theirs was just beginning, in the optimism of a new day, a new project. They had experience. They had commissions.

Hedges and bridges and disconnected pipes and vestigial brick walls were blighted with aerosol doodles, subversive posters: NO 2 WAR. Photographs of photographs of photographs of the very same trees to which the insecure and flapping poster has now been pasted. DANCE ME TO DEATH: the recently dead and the white scarecrows cohabiting in waist-high grass. EAT SHIT, DIE YOUNG.

Here is a torn and abused landscape, kept alive by freelance dealers and wild-eyed wanderers, by revenants and suicides, and even the odd ordinary happy-chatting walker of incontinent dogs. The new stretch was a mirror image of blanket development in the Lea Valley, our mortgaged future. By way of compulsory purchase, compulsory ejection. Conspicuous and unnatural planting schemes and bright blue fences. Old swamps drained, new swamps created. Earthmovers that are not moving. Forests of cranes with flickering warning lights. Artificial herons to keep off the real thing, the spindly predators who might devour the fish that have vanished. Promises and promotions. Revamped smoking sheds. Car giants with 5,000 vehicles ready to go out on choked roads. Culture is coming. Watering holes. Universities. Bars. Faster trains to places nobody wants to go.

When the three peripatetic philosophers walked straight through him for the fourth or fifth time, an impertinent phone was ringing. Something was seriously amiss, out here, with the physics of perception. Two men, the tall one and the troubled one, attached by a long history of engagement, affection and mutual support, had forced the walking dialectic to the point where they were about to come to blows. The peacekeeping nightwalker dropped back, out of range, but close enough to hold the warring couple in view. His pocket was shuddering with voice. He fished the offending instrument out, pressed it to his ear, then handed it over like a hospital pass.

"For you."

The traveller flinched.

"Hello?"

Breathless, in a rush like a single draw from an oxygen flask beginning to run out, words mushed by a rubber mask, and stammering for effect, the voice travelled from a distant place, somewhere like a market bar in Liège, with broken glasses and background hurt. It travelled from wherever is beyond the other side.

"I ne-need a fff-favour. Wha-wha-what does it all mean?"

The traveller whistled. This was a departure. The dead man usually wanted titles of books, details of events he'd quite forgotten.

"It doesn't mean. It just sort of happens. And anyway I should be asking you that now. You had a great funeral, by the way. A couple of moving tributes you probably helped to compose. And famous action, low comedy. Flies around the box. All the wives attending."

The bit the traveller recalled was the last visit, the usual chat, between waves of discomfort, and the reaching out for his hand. That was unusual. There was still warmth in the dying man. "A tender heart," said one of his friends. "He's gone and his work should go with him," said his son. But he wasn't reaching out, he was reaching *through*. There was a half-full glass of beer right behind the visitor, alongside that day's painting, pure abstraction, a bright flush of spidery gestures. The whole scene invigilated by a steady stare from the engraving of Edgar Allan Poe.

171

He handed back the phone, a hot coal. And the three philosophers faded into their own script.

With absolute desolation comes progress, trickle down special offers. The traveller dives into an easy access towpath supermarket, a freezing hangar with light that hurts. He snatches up two bananas and a footballer's drink so sweet his mouth feels immediately diabetic. His throat is a rubbish chute for rotten mangos.

This he has achieved: limbo, free passage through purgatory. And communication, before and after, with those who preceded him. He begins to appreciate the surface of Alba Zutique's photographs. Natural light has abdicated. Fifty-seven varieties of artifice bleed in oil-slick puddles. Bare trees are trapped by their own reflections. The Zeroville hub of High Speed Rail has been betrayed by a set of rubble mountains, pre-wilded green stacks with no animal life. Caffeine headaches from a spouting machine. Crack cocaine. Laughing gas. The lead walker in the troop heading out was vaping like a furnace. White smoke trails hung in the air.

The traveller flips his Lovecraft. The pathology of obsession. The mad hermit scholar in Providence pacing his den, channelling Poe, keeping his back to the window where the creatures scratched. Universal horror exaggerating the mandibular prognathism of an inbred Hapsburg jaw. Language that is hard to chew.

"The effect was that of a Cyclopean city of no architecture known to man or to human imagination, with vast aggregations of night-black masonry embodying monstrous perversions of geometrical laws . . . All these febrile structures seemed knit together by tubular bridges crossing from one to the other at various dizzy heights, and the implied scale of the whole was terrifying and oppressive in its sheer giganticism."

He must be approaching Paddington and the hole in the ground that would send him back east. He willed it. Where was the earth trenched out for this megalomaniac project? Where were the new mountain ranges? Every sandcastle in the Olympic Park affected the psychogeographical balance of London. Every snatch at Lovecraft confirmed prophecy as a set of chyrons, scrolling headlines of doom, running news ticker-tape updates. Bombed cities. Burning towers. Earthquakes. Stabbed children. Missing wives.

At the start of the canal path, out in Northolt, and across from Horsenden Hill, time stretched like a rubber restrainer. There were idyllic English scenes kept safe on the far side of the water. Now Lovecraft's paranoid architecture flooded in, smothering the minutes. Going hard against the elegant curvature of space-time, the traveller was confronted with the terror of entering a text he had already written, but from the wrong end. Undoing everything. Instead of floating into the liberation of Ballard's Westway—"A stone dream that will never awake. As you hurtle along this concrete deck you briefly join the twentieth-century and become a citizen of a virtual city-state borne on a rush of radial tyres"—the traveller hit an imaginary wall. Ballard's looming ramp down which sober citizens, policed by surveillance cameras, held to strict limits, came out of nowhere, huge, dark, a thunder cloud of vertically interred gangsters and redacted visions swollen to nightmare proportions.

He was forced to walk, shuddering, under the long shadow of the concrete whale. The special microclimate beneath motorways once led to enlightenment, traces of survivalist cells, skateboard shamen, booksellers spreading their wares on rugs, under which they would later bunk down for the night. Not now. Not here. This was a penitential crawl-space fit for the latest underclass, for

Portobello Morlocks and those who honoured the local heritage of Michael Moorcock and *Mother London*. This was the lid of a nuclear bunker.

But the traveller was almost there: total disorientation. Elective derangement. He came off at Little Venice. It was too rich, too exotic. Was this the address where Lucian Freud performed his autopsies on living flesh, where he tortured houseplants? And served game from aristocratic estates, rotting and high, to suborned models and daughters. The romance was unbearable. Exploring Venice, even a surrogate version, with a railway map of the London Underground, was a classic Situationist tactic. It felt as if this Venice should be *beyond* Paddington, much closer to St. John's Wood and the zoo. But a shot of Lovecraft, and a swift brandy, put him right. The Rhode Island misogynist grasped how an intimate liaison between the recital of railway halts known to drugged commuters, twinned with trespass beyond forbidden mountain ranges, led to psychotic breakdown and fly-chewing cold-turkey Bram Stoker madness.

"The poor fellow was chanting the familiar stations of the Boston-Cambridge tunnel that burrowed through our peaceful native soil thousands of miles away in New England, yet to me the ritual had neither irrelevance nor home feeling. It had only horror, because I knew unerringly the monstrous, nefandous analogy that had suggested it."

"Nefandous"?

That which must not to be spoken: the unmentionable. And so it was, despite a muttered Elizabeth Line mantra: "Abbey Wood, Woolwich, Custom House, Canary Wharf, Whitechapel, Liverpool Street, Farringdon, Tottenham Court Road, Bond Street (inoperative), Paddington . . . but never on Sundays." Abominable. A sudden chorus of vibrating wings and electrical pulses were necessary accompaniment to the drone of half-completed stations. Pliny the Elder said that the courtship songs of flies are "the opposite of meaningful speech".

The narrator of *At the Mountains of Madness* frames his terrible revelations from Antarctica, filtered by way of Poe's *The Narrative of Arthur Gordon Pym of Nantucket*, stories behind stories, as a warning to the curious. An adventure with deadly consequences, not only for persons foolish enough to broach taboos, but for future generations, for worlds known and unknown, lost and still to come. After the shamanic flight over the cruellest peaks, there was only madness, the straitjacket, cranial intervention by surgical blade or laser beam. The original expedition of Lovecraft's novella only succeeded in activating curses from earlier and verified historic accounts, from geological and cosmological records: metaphors of a mind at the end of its tether, *glimpsing reality*. The thing. The colours out of space.

"It is against my will that I tell my reason for opposing this contemplated invasion of the Antarctic—with its vast fossil hunt and its wholesale boring and melting of ancient ice caps."

Premature ecologist! The narrator confesses everything to deter future violations. On Paddington Station, reaching the shrieked conclusion of Lovecraft's fiction, and rinsing throbbing gums with sour coffee, I saw for an instant the whole picture. Returned to myself, the first person, I was that second expedition, seduced and not repelled by the awful warnings. I was the unwritten afterword to a sensationalist tale of horror, itself filched from the parchment pages of an entirely fraudulent grimoire, held in the library of an obscure New England university. *The Necronomicon*. Now readily available print-on-demand from Tasmania.

Achieving at last the glorious high-Soviet down escalator to the Elizabeth Line—like a super-Palladium set of stairs (out of the 1946 Powell and Pressburger film, *A Matter of Life and Death*), slipway to Hell, not stairway to Heaven—I made the best of an empty platform. It was as long as the deck of an aircraft carrier. Sliding glass doors kept suicides from the electrified tracks. Arrival times were visible and changing. I had three minutes to finish with Lovecraft.

The analogue to "things that should not be" was "a vast, onrushing subway train as one sees it from a station platform—the great black front looming colossally out of infinite subterranean distance, constellated with strangely coloured lights and filling the prodigious burrow as a piston fills a cylinder."

This was a cathartic conclusion I could not indulge. Because I had already shared it, many years ago, in an incident reported as "The Cleansing of Angels". Steampunk Victoriana. Old railways, failed speculations. Ancient crimes. "The eye of the rapidly approaching monster filled the tunnel: it was scarlet, a steppewolf dribbling fire . . . The engine was no machine, but a living thing. It was cloaked in vegetation, it was live; rich with veins and secret leaves . . . Streams of clear water ran from its side."

Old visions without context. Old London nightmares.

"But we were not on a station platform," Lovecraft wrote. "We were on the track ahead as the nightmare, plastic column of fetid black iridescence oozed tightly onward through its fifteen-foot sinus, gathering unholy speed and driving before it a spiral, rethickening cloud of the pallid abyss vapor . . . a terrible, indestructible thing vaster than any subway train—a shapeless congeries of protoplasmic bubbles, faintly self-luminous, and with myriads of temporary eyes forming and un-forming as pustules of greenish light."

I was saved from my own nightmares by upgraded safety protocols, the sliding doors that would not allow me on to the edge of the platform with that vision into the howl and hiss of the approaching train with its myriads of eyes, its watching wings, its bloody tongue licking at an imaginary bowl, hollowed from the skull of William Blake. Rigid on my bench, on the deserted platform, I understood the projected image as an image. And I fled.

Beelzebub of the railway! Baal of the tunnels! Leather fetish hood and strap-on wings for display only in lightless labyrinths of fugitive railway-arch clubs and secret state storage facilities. Ghost platforms shared with "plague-ridden" cannibal troglodytes, ancestors of buried construction gangs. *Ba'al-zabûb: Lord of the Flies!* Engine of destiny. Your captive cultists are feasting on flies feasting on excrement. Prince of Demons, recognised by Milton, revised by Blake! Lord of the Flies! The great fly mask, made from thousands of lesser things, from the sticky corpses slaughtered on Machen's treacle-smeared newspaper, shines in the velvet darkness of the Elizabeth Line tunnel. Inky with newsprint, flies compose obscene odes on cracked ceilings. Pregnant with future headlines, they shape-shift. But not into other species of insect or plague bacilli, but into human form. Our brothers, our shadow selves. "It has a heart like thee, a brain open to heaven & hell, with inside wondrous & expansive; its gates are not clos'd." As Blake knew. And saw.

And Beckett too, in the purgatory of his London delirium, always on the tramp to nowhere, monkey-hill to Tower Bridge. He confesses to a filial relationship: "My brother the fly / the common housefly / sidling out of darkness into light . . . it is the autumn of his life / he could not serve typhoid and mammon."

I fled the voices and the compound eye. I rode the escalator through its gallery of floral trash to the showy entrance hall, the closed gates eating credit, the chaos dance of the great station concourse with its tamed and anxious travellers. Myigros: he who chases flies. I was done. Talked out in my stubborn silence.

There was a book barge in Paddington Basin. Better by far to walk home beside the water, absorbed in its slow and steady murmur. Soft streets and white avenues of Marylebone: "The fields from Islington to Marybone, / To Primrose Hill and Saint John's Wood, / Were builded over with pillars of gold, /And there Jerusalem's pillars stood." A short step, then, to settle back to former habits and beliefs, in order to make connection with the urban swagger of the Regent's Canal. The bellow of the bison. The scream of the macaw. The growl of the meat-breathed lion. The gibbering of apes. This barge was known to Stewart Lee. It was run by a charitable man. I could dump my Lovecraft into his safekeeping. And walk away.

Paddington was not safe territory. It was known to the Great Beast, to Crowley. More fly than man, he paraded Praed Street in the service of his secret masters. He sauntered, he prowled for dung to be exchanged for gold. He availed himself, in the days of his inheritance, of common prostitutes. Who were disposable, but never common. Who had energies on which he could draw. Who had lives and biographies that meant nothing to him. A surfeit of class vanity sustained the Beast. He found one of his own volumes maligned in a pornographic bookshop, a dirty-windowed cave out of Conrad's *The Secret Agent*. He demanded consequences, legal restitution. And a compliant English judiciary, fellow Masons, obliged. But Crowley did not know my home ground. He barely ventured beyond Islington. It was terra incognita. It had its resident demons. "Walk to Haggerston Town Hall," he wrote in 1909, "wherever Haggerston may be." He was never out there, on foot. He dodged the required period of Hackney initiation and moved straight to Hastings. Heroin and mutton.

The gangplank was down, choice items sweated in a tarry sunset. "I remember you," the bookman said. "You came aboard, in a thunderstorm with double rainbows, to give a talk about . . . where was it? Peru? Nobody turned up. I do remember that."

Books and water are troublesome bedfellows. The neatly arranged ranks, set out to attract the mothers or keepers of restless weekend children, and sentimental bibliophiles who stroke but do not buy, were so much ballast. Green smoke for the woodstove on a winter night. Damp insulation. The books were not happy. Out on the ocean, beyond the hope of land, they would settle to their fate, pawed at by salty fingers stinking of fish. Here it was painful. Décor of provisional enlightenment. Talked about, perhaps, never activated.

I thought of George Gissing, an author from the grubby streets, clerk, scholar, misguided lover, and failed thief. He knew the warmth of libraries. He knew what it was to starve at the desk. Bookcases filled with taunts, with weight and tonnage, were alps he would never conquer. The centre of the British Library, under the dome, is the centre of everything. "The readers who sat here at these radiating lines of desks, what were they but hapless flies caught in a huge web, its nucleus the great circle of the Catalogue? Darker, darker."

Fill the docket. Make your claim. Summon the pirated vanities of Crowley from a locked cabinet. You've got the Latin for it and the Greek. Phil Baker in his meticulous tour of the Great Beast's London geography, his book made from books and boots, identified all the relevant places of domicile. Crimes were indulged and briskly summarised. He quotes Robert Irwin: "One thing you can say about Satanists, they are great readers."

According to Baker, Crowley said that there was a period in his life, the time when he wrote the "Proem" to his play *The World's Tragedy*, when his style could be identified as pure "Paddington". A nice conceit, place leaking into line breaks, into an excess of commas, into language. Flirtatious, cautious, proud as a pimp.

If it has not been read, it didn't happen. If it has not been read, it was never written. If it has been written, it will never go away. If these events did happen in a written landscape, they must stop where that landscape runs out. If they stop, there is no more, of book or writer or place. I take out my Lovecraft, give a wipe to the already gleaming cover, and admire for the last time the imagined—and therefore immortal—architecture, that thrusting phallic tower of quotations, as heaped and time-collaged as Nicholas Hawksmoor's vertiginous Christ Church in old Spitalfields. The stack looming over crouching aliens.

The boatman is charitable, kind to the undeserving and the deserving alike. He accepts the dubious offering and allows me to take my pick from the tray of "recent acquisitions" that he is putting outside, to tempt the pre-literate and the vulgarly curious.

How nearly I succumb to the respectable block of the *Buildings of England. London 3: North West* by Bridget Cherry and Nikolaus Pevsner. I pick it up. I try to scroll back to the start of this day's impossible walk by searching out Hillingdon.

"Hillingdon, on the fringe of the built-up area of London, is one of the largest of the outer London boroughs and has some of the most extreme architectural contrasts to be found anywhere in London." Very true: if you navigate by manmade structures, their dates and their details. "A flat, noisy plain dominated by motorways and airport."

Nick Papadimitriou, solitary, scavenging, and open to queer addictive currents, has more poetry. More investment in the territory of his heart. He will walk the towpath and the hard shoulder forever.

Pevsner has a note on "Perambulations". "A tour should start in the churchyard." Good advice. Start and finish. Ashes scattered in the shadow of a yew, older than history, while the deceased is still flinching from some "characteristically tactless sixties office block" or "deliberately friendly vernacular image replacing the short-lived brutalist tower built for BEA in 1964".

The Pevsner was worthy, a potential future resource, but too heavy for my rucksack. And that future, unwritten, was already used up. There was no way I could work a few lines of the German pedant into my overstuffed and massively overspiced broth. Better to accept, without comment, the slim proof copy the boatman offered. He was keen, I remembered the syndrome only too well, to get shot of an unsalable item, lacking a decent come-on cover image.

"Time-coded at two hours and forty minutes after he died, I received a message on my duncephone from the poet and painter whose work and presence had affected all our lives."

An awkward opening. Too precise in its notation of time, trying to convince by a display of hard evidence. But I might give it a spin. Ready to forget but not forgive. Someone once told me that the dead are permitted to come back three times. More often they will email their posthumous dreams. That recent poet was a sticker. He walked in my sleep, out to Stoke Newington, and "through a dark, bombed-out London house". He was carrying a gift in a plastic bag. It looked like a drowning fairground goldfish. "I'll always be there for you." And he was. Beyond what was written. Or what could be written. Beyond memories trapped without password in an inherited laptop.

Unfit to take the argument further, the traveller was ready to move out, and to walk. On and on and on and on and on. Until the bookman's phone trilled and he listened and nodded and handed it to me. "For you." And, like the agent of a footballer's wife disposing of inconvenient evidence, I dropped it straight over the side. Down through the thick green mantle. Gone. And I did walk. On and on and on and on and on. On this side of the grass, there is nothing else.

Acknowledgements

The trigger for these overlapping stories came when Richard Frame invited me to contribute a Machen associated piece to a new collection to be published by Three Imposters. *House of Flies* behaved like necessary dictation. I'm grateful to Three Imposters for permission to include the resulting story in this Swan River cluster.

With the flies in active occupation, the other stories followed in quick succession. *London Spirit* began, in a quite different iteration, as a response to a Ballard invitation from Rick McGrath and Maxim Jakubowski. But Machen insisted on joining that one too.

The elegant productions from Swan River, both rescued and original texts, have long been an inspiration. I especially admired the presentation by Brian J. Showers of B. Catling's *Munky*. A book to which I return, time and again; with particular memories of a canoe trip from Oxford to Dorchester-on-Thames.

My thanks to everybody at Swan River, especially Brian J. Showers, instigator and enabler. As will be obvious, I owe so much here to the work and company, actual and imagined, of Alan Moore, Michael Moorcock, B. Catling, Steve Moore, Stewart Lee, Andrew Kötting, J. G. Ballard, Effie Paleologou. And special thanks, yet again, to Dave McKean for his graphic interpretations and magical illuminations; and to Joy Gordon for the author photo. And the late, continuing, and remarkable Paris-based bookman/musician, Martin Stone.

About the Author

Iain Sinclair has lived in Hackney since 1968, working at a variously titled London project. He has published widely through mainstream and independent presses. These crimes have been comprehensively collected in a three-volume bibliography/biography by Jeff Johnson. Now published by Test Centre Books. An early prose-poetry trilogy was followed by the novels *Downriver* and *Radon Daughters*. The short-story collection, *Slow Chocolate Autopsy*, was a first collaboration with Dave McKean. Sinclair was formerly a used-book dealer and never quite got over it.

About the Illustrator

Dave McKean has illustrated and designed many ground breaking books and graphic novels including *The Magic of Reality* (Richard Dawkins), *The Homecoming* (Ray Bradbury), *The Savage* (David Almond), *What's Welsh for Zen* (John Cale), *Arkham Asylum* (Grant Morrison) and *Mr. Punch*, *Wolves in the Walls*, *Coraline*, and *The Graveyard Book* (Neil Gaiman). He wrote and illustrated *Pictures That Tick*, *Black Dog: The Dreams of Paul Nash* and the multi-award winning *Cages*. He has created hundreds of CD and comic covers including the entire run of Gaiman's *Sandman*. He has directed five short and three feature films, *MirrorMask*, *Luna*, and *The Gospel of Us* with Michael Sheen.

SWAN RIVER PRESS

Founded in 2003, Swan River Press is an independent
publishing company, based in Dublin, Ireland, dedicated
to gothic, supernatural, and fantastic literature. We special-
ise in limited edition hardbacks, publishing fiction from
around the world with an emphasis on Ireland's contribu-
tions to the genre.

www.swanriverpress.ie

*"Handsome, beautifully made volumes . . .
altogether irresistible."*

– Michael Dirda, *Washington Post*

*"It [is] often down to small, independent, specialist presses
to keep the candle of horror fiction flickering . . . "*

– Darryl Jones, *Irish Times*

"Swan River Press—cutting edge of New Gothic."

– Joyce Carol Oates

*"The redoubtable Brian J. Showers [keeps] the
myriad voices of Irish fantasy alive there in Dublin."*

– Alan Moore

MUNKY

B. Catling

When the puckish spirit of a monk begins haunting the storied village of Pulborough, known for its ancient abbey, Maud Garner, manager of the Coach and Horses Inn, arranges for the famous ghost hunter, Walter Prince, to come investigate. And from there, things spiral out of control.

Peopled with richly drawn Dickensian grotesques and filled with bizarre and comical incident, *Munky* is as compelling as it is antic. Catling transports the reader to an interwar England in the throes of change. Part bizarre ghost story, part whimsical farce, part idiosyncratic literary experiment, it could be described as P. G. Wodehouse collaborating with Raymond Roussel, with a dash of M. R. James, if it weren't so uniquely its own thing.

> *"Munky is a delirious blend*
> *of terror and pantomime."*

– Iain Sinclair

> *"Brian Catling is simply a genius. His writing is*
> *so extraordinary it hurts, makes me realise*
> *how little imagination I have."*

– Terry Gilliam

> *"It's a glorious creepy world that*
> *Brian creates and inhabits."*

– Alan Moore

THE HOUSE ON
THE BORDERLAND

William Hope Hodgson

An exiled recluse, an ancient abode in the remote west of Ireland, nightly attacks by malevolent swine-things from a nearby pit, and cosmic vistas beyond time and space. *The House on the Borderland* has been praised by China Miéville, Terry Pratchett, and Clark Ashton Smith, while H. P. Lovecraft wrote, "Few can equal [Hodgson] in adumbrating the nearness of nameless forces and monstrous besieging entities through casual hints and significant details, or in conveying feelings of the spectral and abnormal."

"Almost from the moment that you hear the title," observes Alan Moore, "you are infected by the novel's weird charisma. Knock and enter at your own liability." *The House on the Borderland* remains one of Hodgson's most celebrated works. This new edition features an introduction by Alan Moore, an afterword by Iain Sinclair, and illustrations by John Coulthart.

*"A summit of Cosmic horror.
Scary, disturbing and magical."*

– Guillermo del Toro

*"Swan River Press has produced the best version ever.
There is no need for any other."*

– *Dead Reckonings*

THE SATYR & OTHER TALES

Stephen J. Clark

In the final throes of the Blitz, Austin Osman Spare is the only salvation for Marlene, an artist escaping a traumatic past. Wandering Southwark's ruins she encounters Paddy Hughes, a fugitive of another kind. Falling under Marlene's spell Hughes agrees to seek out her lost mentor, the man she calls The Satyr. Yet Marlene's past will not rest as the mysterious Doctor Charnock pursues them, trying to capture the patient she'd once caged. *The Satyr* is a tale inspired by the life and ethos of sorcerer and artist Austin Osman Spare.

Another three novellas of occult enchantment follow: a bookseller discovers that his late wife knew the Devil, in the Carpathian Mountains refugees shelter in a museum devoted to a forgotten author, and in Prague a portraitist must paint a countess whose appearance is never the same twice.

"This book will adorn your shelves, where it will be at ease in shadowy converse with your copies of À Rebours, The Picture of Dorian Gray, The Great God Pan."

– Mark Valentine

"Clark's subtle prose, vivid and disturbing imagery, and the concepts he weaves into his stories make them irresistible to those whose senses have been jaded by more common fare."

– *Black Static*

Milton Keynes UK
Ingram Content Group UK Ltd.
UKHW010944090124
435730UK00004B/149